HEALING CHOICE

CHOOSE YOUR FATE

SUSI HAWKE

Editing provided by Jill Wexler, LesCourt Author Services

Proofreading by Lori Parks, LesCourt Author Services

Cover design by Ana J Phoenix

PROLOGUE

I had been sitting in my bedroom, minding my own business and wondering what I was going to do with myself if I left the family business, when a bright light flashed. I sat up and gazed in wonder as the familiar swirling colors of the old, long-forgotten portal to the human realm appeared not three meters from my bed.

Since there was nothing to do but explore this bit of fun, I slipped on my shoes and a clean shirt before stepping into the inviting, glittery blur of light and color. After so much time, I had forgotten the out-of-body feeling it gave me as if it were realigning all my atoms and molecules just milliseconds prior to the half-snap of the fingers it took to step through it from one side to the other.

As soon as my feet touched onto the dewy grass in the predawn chill, I noticed a group of men—shifters—dropping their hands and stepping apart while the portal blinked into non-existence.

I stood there, blinking around at this circle I had fallen into when an old, familiar face greeted me with a ready smile. "Greetings, Tobias. Welcome back to the mortal realm;

it's only been an eon or two since you left, but you'll find that much has changed in that time."

With a brief nod, I glanced around to smile at each of the men who had brought me here as I answered my prince. "Aye, Easton. 'Tis good to be here again. Does this mean the treaty has been severed?"

The portal had been sealed with the signing of a treaty that kept both my kind, and that of the gods, from freely walking this human realm. Too much blood had been spilled in the war between the gods and Fae over the fledgling human race for anything else to have worked. Only the removal of immortals from their world gave the mortals a chance to live freely—especially given the evil natures of the Unseelie court who had loved to drink human blood and use them as their puppets. Not that we Seelies were much better, charming and beguiling the poor shites out of anything and everything we had wanted from them. I had not blamed the ancient shamen who had conspired with the goddess to lock us all way.

Easton shook his head in answer to my question. "No. What it means is that the goddess Artio has decided to give a few of our kind a second chance in this realm. We Fae are seldom given a shot at true love, aye? What would you say if I were to offer you such a gift?"

"I would ask what you wanted in return or what you were peddling, Easton. Nobody does something of that magnitude without seeking recompense." I shot Easton a knowing grin as I chuckled.

"Sure, and I wouldn't blame you for thinking that. However, the goddess has an offer for you," Easton answered with a grin.

"For me? What makes *me* so special that a goddess would take notice of the likes of me?" I shifted my weight onto one hip, crossing my arms over my chest to hear what Easton had to say.

A soft-spoken man answered instead. "The goddess is making the offer, but our circle here has the sole responsibility for this venture. We've peered into your realm and watched you and your fellow Fae as you've gone about your lives to live, work, and play. The reason you caught our eye was because you did a kindness for a child not too long ago. She had no food and was begging for coins. What did you do? You emptied your pockets and gave her all your gold. That kind act alone told us everything we needed to know about your nature. That's why we've chosen you to be the first to be offered this opportunity."

I felt my cheeks flushing as I looked down at my feet. "Hailee is but a wee bairn. She lost both of her parents to an attack by the Unseelie a few months ago, and lives with her elderly grandmother. The two of them beg for coins and food just to survive. It is not right, and besides, I only did what anyone would do."

"No, you did what any person with a decent heart would do." Another voice spoke firmly. "None of the other Fae who passed that child had even bothered to give her so much as a coin. Yet you gave her everything you had to give."

The one who seemed to be running the show, based on his cocky stance and attitude, waved a hand as he smirked. "So now that we've established that you're a good guy, would you care to know what we're here to offer you?"

"Yes, please. Although, if I am being honest—it is gift enough to just be back in this realm." I hoped that my sincere smile confirmed that they had made the right choice in offering me this rare and special gift.

"Allow me to explain." The man held up a hand as he spoke. "The goddess would like to offer you a chance to meet

3

your heartsong. The one person in this realm that would complete you. The yin to your yang, as it were."

Oh, I was definitely intrigued now and nodded eagerly. "And you can introduce me to this person who shares my heartsong?"

Another of their circle shook his head. "No, we are limited in how much we are allowed to be involved. You and you alone will hear your true mate's heartsong, no matter where they are in our world. Go to them and make them fall in love with you of their own accord." He glanced around their circle and they shared what looked like nervous smiles before reciting an obviously rehearsed rhyme.

"Find your mate and choose your fate
    You've thirty days and don't be late
    No majicks or tricks, nor cheat or spell
    Conceal you're Fae and hide it well
    Should your heartsong find something amiss
    You can reveal all after love's true kiss"

After they had finished, I nodded thoughtfully. "I can work with that. But tell me, what is the catch? Trust me, there is always a catch..."

Easton threw his head back with a boisterous laugh. "Sure, and ain't that the truth? We gave you the catch in the second line, laddie. You only have thirty days in this realm to find your heartsong and make them fall for you. On the thirtieth day, the two of you must return here by sunset to meet with us. At that point, you will both be given a choice."

I tipped my head curiously as I gazed at my prince. "And what exactly would that choice entail?"

One of the men smiled as he gently explained. "Here's the

thing. You know the treaty says that you can't stay in this realm as a Fae, and biology won't allow your heartsong to return as a mortal with you. As a couple, you will need to choose one realm or the other. Should you decide to stay here, you will give up your Fae majicks and become a shifter like us. You'll have the same lifespan as your mate, and you can pick the spirit animal of your choice. Should the two of you decide to return to your world, your mate will exchange their soul for immortality so that they may join you there. Whichever choice the two of you make will be final; you'll need to be prepared for that."

I whistled through my teeth as the enormity of that proposition settled in my head. It would be difficult, but gads, would the payoff be worth it. "That is quite a task and much to ask of anybody, especially when I cannot tell them my secrets. I am willing to try though. It will be worth the effort if it means I will have my heartsong."

"Good luck to you." A small, quiet man who had been watching our conversation smiled and bowed his head.

"We'll be rooting for you both," another man added.

"But don't screw up and break any rules, because Easton and the goddess will also be watching," another new voice warned.

"And above all, don't forget to let your heartsong know that they're everything to you," a tall omega with friendly eyes suggested as a helpful hint.

My head tipped to the side as the most beautiful sound I had ever heard hit my ears and spoke straight to my soul. I was already twitching to go as I looked around the circle again. "That part about no majicks, did it go into effect the minute I stepped into this realm, or can I maybe whisk myself across the globe to where I can already hear the song of my heart?"

"We'll allow it," the soft-spoken man said with a smile.

5

"We will also allow you to change your clothes to blend in and maybe consider a concealing spell to hide your wings and pointed ears." Another of the men grinned as he gestured toward my appearance. "You're not allowed to use majicks to affect or trick your heartsong, but there are no rules about using it to transport yourself or blend into your surroundings. Not to mention the small issue of getting food, clothes, and lodging. Use your Fae majicks carefully though; if you take advantage and break any of our rules, you'll lose your chance to be with your heartsong forever."

"You do not have to worry about that." I smiled, probably too eagerly, as I took a step to the side, leaning in the direction of that delicious heartsong.

"Get on with it then." Easton stepped aside to break the circle so I could pass. "The clock has already started ticking— we'll see you again in thirty days."

As I rushed out of the circle, scampering off into the night and blinking out of their view as I snapped an invisibility spell over myself, I heard Easton's voice behind me, giving me a reminder that they would be watching. "This is going to be so much fun; I can't wait to see what happens next."

1

TOBIAS

*M*y head was spinning from the amazing opportunity that had just fallen into my lap. To have a mate, and not just any mate but a true mate—the actual melody that would complete my heartsong—it was too incredible for words.

As I raced off in a blur of winged magic, I almost instantly crossed an ocean, a sprawling continent, and more populated areas than I would have guessed existed before I finally tuned in on the exact location of my mate. I was barely aware of the light changing as I went from night to day in a matter of moments.

I cloaked myself in an invisibility charm—a handy bit of majick—before I lowered myself to the ground and walked over the dusty road that led to a large city spread over a desert valley.

A cacophony of noises washed over me, along with the foul, mechanical stench of the strange metallic carriages that zoomed and zipped past me. One particular carriage, which was both longer and taller than my home, caught the corner of my wing and sent me spinning a few meters into the desert like a whirling dervish.

When I had caught my balance, I stood there with a hand clutched over my heart as I watched the monstrosities race by. Holding a hand over my eyes to block the sun, I blinked a few times as I stared at a sign on the outskirts of town. I pulled on my majicks to help me decipher the words—Welcome to Las Vegas.

Aye, and what a welcome it was... I took a step toward the sign and nearly got smashed by yet another metallic beast. Obviously, I needed to figure out what was going on and fast; or I would not live long enough to make it to my mate's side.

My wings fluttered with a mere thought, lifting me high into the air where I was safely out of danger from the roadway. A rumbling sound caught my ear and I looked to the side to see another kind of carriage. This one was a true behemoth, and it was flying right at me! The brute shocked me so much that I nearly flew into a cement bridge that crossed the maniacal roadway.

What sort of majicks had the humans concocted that they could make winged carriages that flew through the air? I hovered over the bridge like a hummingbird as I yielded the airspace to the enormous blue carriage. The word Southwest was written proudly along its flank and its brightly colored tail would rival any peacock.

I needed more information, and quickly. Once I could safely proceed, I darted off and headed toward what looked like the heart of the city. I lowered myself to the ground on the main thoroughfare, getting close enough to read minds and absorb knowledge from a mob of people walking past one of the glittering palatial structures that lined either side of the boulevard.

Despite the fact that it was late afternoon by my best estimate, several of the minds I attempted to read were already either inebriated or stoned on some substance or other. It took me several minutes I could barely spare before I was able to find a quick mind filled with knowledge. I was gobsmacked by what I was learning as I rifled through the person's memory and absorbed their cultural knowledge as my own.

After I had gleaned memories and sifted through several minds, I had learned enough to understand this strange new world. I could not help but be impressed. Humanity had certainly come a long way since I had last seen them. Now that I understood what cars and planes were, I was able to safely flit across the city to where my heartsong cried out like a beacon.

I found myself in an industrial area on the far side of the city when I finally reached the area where my mate awaited me. Keeping the cloak of invisibility tightly around myself, I decided to watch my mate for a bit to get better acquainted before I decided how best to proceed with my wooing.

When I saw her, the small woman with long, coppery red hair flowing down her back, I was caught up short. I did not care that my mate was a woman—gender was never an issue for me where attraction was concerned—but I was caught off guard by the fact that she was walking a small white wolf on a leash through the urban parking area.

I could sense the shifter magic without even trying, and it was enough to make me pause and rethink this for a moment. Could I be with somebody who would be so cruel as to leash a shifter like a pet? Surely she knew what he was, how could she not?

Although, maybe she *was* unaware. From the one shifter mind I had happened upon during my travels across town, I had picked up on the fact that they kept their animal side a secret from the rest of their society. Which made sense to me, as humans had never done well with anything different than themselves. It was a sad fact of life.

Walking a little faster, I dodged through the parked cars to get a closer look. My intention was to touch the shifter's mind and see if the poor soul was being leashed against their will or merely keeping their shifter status a secret from my mate for some reason or other. My heart raced when I got closer and realized that the woman was not my mate after all. It was the wolf!

Indignation rose in my chest, making my heart pound with rage. I was about to reveal myself right then and there, and remove the head of the wench who would dare leash my mate, when she stopped mid-step and rested a hand on my mate's head. She bent beside him to whisper in his ear. "Are you sure you're up to this, Caleb? I know you want to help these people. But you really don't have to, hon."

Caleb. I rolled the name around my mind, finding pleasure in its sound. My mate's name was Caleb. I stretched a hand out without thinking, as if to run my hand over the soft-looking fur, when his tail swung to the side and slapped my hand away. Caleb looked back over his shoulder, his whiskey brown eyes searching to see the presence he clearly felt. He was sniffing the air with one ear perked up as if he could hear me but before he could react any further, the woman gave a tug to his leash and grumbled about getting on with things as she led him inside the building.

2

CALEB

*A*s Helena walked me into the back room, I could hear the rustling noises and murmurs of the crowd that waited on the other side of the curtain while Madame Diane finished her question and answer session. Normally I'd be excited and ready to do my part to save as many lives as I could, but I couldn't focus today. I'd been hearing a faint melodic sound since I opened my eyes this morning. But even as I puzzled over it, the music hadn't truly distracted me until we'd been in the parking lot just now.

Not only could I hear the music as if it were standing next to me—a strange musicality that seemed to echo the beats of my heart—but I could almost feel it. I kept looking around, expecting to see someone standing there, but it must have only been in my mind. It wasn't until I heard the click of the leash unfastening that I realized that Helena was getting us ready to perform.

She knelt in front of me, taking a soft brush out of her bag to brush my fur and make me look as appealing and nonthreatening as was possible. I made a chuffing noise when she pulled out the bright turquoise bandanna that she insisted on tying around my neck.

"Oh, hush. What if there are children in the lineup today? Hmm? Don't you want them to think you're approachable? Trust me, hon. Between this bandanna and a few innocent tail wags, you'll have them eating out of your hand—or paw, I should say." Helena's eyes twinkled as she spoke. I'd never called her out on it, but I was pretty sure she took perverse pleasure in teasing me when I was in my animal form and couldn't talk back.

I satisfied myself with nipping at the hairbrush, but Helena was too fast and pulled away to tuck it back into her bag before I could get my teeth wrapped around it. One of the stagehands glanced our way. "Are you about ready, ma'am? The healer is done giving her speech, so you and the dog will be up next."

Helena rolled her eyes with suppressed mirth as he turned away. We'd been working with Madame Diane for months now. If we didn't have the routine down cold by now, I'd be concerned for our intelligence. For the benefit of any humans watching, Helena shot me an apologetic smile before patting the side of her leg and making a kissing sound. "You heard him, boy. Come on, now. Come, boy. Let's go sniff out some disease, shall we?" I played along, wagging my tail as I moved to her side and allowed her to lead me onto the stage as the curtains opened.

We walked across the stage to the pair of red velvet, throne-like chairs where Helena would sit with me at her side while our potential patients sat across from us. It was hard to focus and I was distracted from truly noticing the full house of people. That odd music was following me. Now it was as if someone were playing it right at my side.

Shit. Maybe it wasn't music at all. Was this a new symptom? Dammit, I wasn't ready yet. I still had work to do and people to save.

Helena sat in the chair, arranging her voluminous skirts artfully over her lap while I sat back on my haunches beside her. Helena smiled at the crowd, lifting a hand to wave while resting the other on my head and scratching between my ears.

Her broad smile was firmly in place as she hissed between her teeth, knowing full well that I'd hear every word. "I don't like this, Caleb. I feel like this is too much for you today. There are too many people. You need to be home resting. Your aura was a mess today. You can't help others by killing yourself, hon."

I sniffed and turned my head in the direction of the first person being led onto the stage. As much as I appreciated Helena's concern, I wasn't going to stop just yet. Even if this was my last day working, and I only found one person in this entire auditorium who'd been helped by my enhanced skills —it would be enough to make whatever time I had left on earth worthwhile.

The first potential patient was a middle-aged woman. I could smell the cancer before she even took her seat. And that right there was why I was here. I waited for Helena to get her permission for me to examine her, before standing on all four paws and walking in a circle around the chair.

Even though I didn't need to drag it out, there was a certain amount of showmanship that the people seemed to need in order to believe what Helena had to tell them. Once the woman began to calm and accept my presence, I made a show of sniffing around her arms and abdomen before pushing my nose directly against the uppermost part of the outer area of her left breast.

As I pointed to the area where the cancer was located, I raised my paw as if to shake hands and batted the air twice.

Helena watched for the signal and quietly informed the woman that I was detecting Stage II breast cancer. Helena was already passing her a tissue when tears began to fall down the woman's face.

Ignoring the tissue, she wrapped her arms around my neck instead, crying against my fur while she whimpered in my ear. "Thank you, dear heart. The tests the doctors ran were inconclusive, but now I'll go for a second opinion. My mother died of breast cancer, and I'll be damned if I rob my children of their mother if I can help it."

Madame Diane, the healer, came forward to escort the woman off to the side for a private conversation while Helena and I waited for the next patient to approach. Thankfully, the next dozen or so people were all cancer free. All it took was a wag of my tail as I stepped back for Helena to give them the good news.

As each person was led away by one of Madame Diane's assistants, they were given a pamphlet on clean eating and offered the option of purchasing crystals for additional protection. I ignored that part of the process because I was already moving on to the next person.

It went fairly quickly when there was no cancer involved, but when I detected tumors, we had to give the person a moment to accept the news. I was getting my hopes up that maybe this session would go faster than most, when a young man in his late twenties approached. I groaned mentally, already knowing how awkward this one was going to go. After I made a show of circling his chair and sniffing him, moving as slowly as I could because I could practically taste the fear coming off him in waves, I forced myself to step right between his legs and plunged my nose forward.

I could hear by Helena's muted gasp that she knew exactly where I was going. Yeah, prostate cancer diagnoses were never easy. I was just glad that nobody could see me blush in this form as I wedged my nose between the man's balls and the seat. As soon as Helena had correctly spotted how many times I wave my paw, I took a respectful step back and licked the man's hand where it rested on his knee.

I hated for him to hear such awful news while fighting his natural fear of me, so I did my part to play up the *I'm an adorable puppy dog* act. Anyone who knew better would know that I was a wolf—not a house dog—but I did my best to play my role.

After the young man was led away, the next three people were also cancer patients. After them, I had a break when the next couple dozen people were all cancer free. Strangely, the odd music I kept hearing was giving me the strength to persevere. Too bad it was probably just another symptom of my ever decreasing longevity.

My spirit stayed strong, despite the few patients where I detected tumors that I knew in my heart were untreatable— until I had to sniff a child. An adorable little boy who wasn't even big enough to climb up into the chair, but had to be lifted by his mother, made my heart break in two because I could smell the leukemia on his breath. Dammit.

With children, I took a little longer to set them at ease. Licking their hands, letting them pull on my ears, roughly pet my head—or in this little tyke's case, even slap his palms on my cheeks as he shrieked "good doggy" in my face. He was too cute for words, despite the fact that he was blasting my eardrums with his shrill little voice.

Even if he hadn't been so adorable, I'd have happily let him do his worst rather than have to share what I smelled. Using our sign for leukemia, I carefully sniffed along his arm while waving my paw. I played with him for a few minutes, letting him smack the top of my head in his childish attempt to pet me while Helena gave his parents the bad news.

It was just my luck that the next few people were also

cancer patients. My head was starting to buzz and I could feel the tremors starting in my limbs as I grew dizzy but I forced myself to finish the last few people who had waited so patiently for their own turn with Frosty the Cancer Sniffing Canine.

As soon as the last person was being led away—thankfully, cancer free—I flopped down onto the stage as my vision blurred and the darkness pulled me under.

.

TOBIAS

*W*hen Caleb hit the floor, it was as though his life force had suddenly been snuffed like a candle. I whisked a quick glamour over myself, retracting my wings and rounding the tips of my ears to a more human look and dropped my invisibility cloak when nobody was paying attention.

The woman who had been working with my mate was kneeling at his side, shaking his limp body and crying his name. Despite all he had just done for the people present, nobody sprang forward to assist. The people who worked with the healer woman were busy selling their crystals to the remaining customers, and the healer herself was deep in conversation with the parents of the sick boy he had diagnosed with that neat trick he had been doing.

When I suddenly appeared and dropped down next to my mate, the woman did a double take and looked around quickly as she clutched at her chest. "Where did you come from? Holy bazookas, you scared the life out of me, buddy. Sorry, my dog is sick. We're done for the day, you'll have to catch us next time."

Ignoring her, I rested a hand on his head and suddenly discovered the truth. My mate was sick himself. I could easily see it in my mind's eye, but the information came from the woman's head about the glioblastoma in his parietal lobe. Instantly absorbing the facts, I understood in a flash that my mate would not last much longer in this world.

When the woman started to shake him harder, I clutched her hands and made her look me in the eye. "That will not rouse him, he has worn himself out. Allow me to carry him for you, if you will?"

She bit her lip hesitantly, but she clearly was not up to the task of lifting a wolf, even one as small as Caleb. I could not help but respect the concern I read in her mind about trusting a stranger with her dear friend. In that moment, I knew that I liked her. I smiled and lightened my hold on her hands. "I am sorry, I have been very rude. Allow me to introduce myself? My name is Tobias of the Coppersmith clan. Would you allow me to be of assistance, please?"

I realized I had made a mistake when she frowned at my full name. A quick read of her mind told me that Coppersmith by itself would have been more palatable. I stared into her eyes, sending a magical compulsion for her to trust me. A brief flash of worry hit me then as I remembered the rules— until I realized that I had inadvertently found a loophole.

The rules said that I could not reveal myself to my mate; they had said nothing about using compulsion on his human friend. For that matter, there was nothing saying I could not compel myself right into their lives—as long as my mate was unaware, no rules would be broken.

She responded instantly to the compulsion, the tension in her shoulders relaxing as a beautiful smile spread over her almost elfin face. "Forgive me, Tobias of the Coppersmith clan. I get a little protective when it comes to Caleb. My name is Helena Rushing, and this is my friend Caleb Beardsley. And thank you for the kind offer. Yes, I think I would be grateful if you could give me a hand. I'd like to get him home where he can rest."

"I am pleased to assist." I nodded solemnly and released her hands as I stood then bent to lift Caleb in my arms. I followed her out to the parking lot, unsurprised to see that the sun was setting. My poor mate had been in there for far too many hours. He must have personally scented over two hundred people; it was surely a testament to his strength of will that he had made it through the entire assembly.

Helena led me to a red and white utility vehicle that had the word Blazer written on the back end. *What was with this human need to name their modes of transportation?* She lifted the door for me to settle Caleb into the storage compartment.

I started to crawl in next to him but she stopped me with a hand to my shoulder. "Oh, no, dear. You'll have to ride up front with me. The last thing I need is to be pulled over because an officer spotted you sitting in the back with no seatbelt while I'm transporting what would appear to be a wolf. Caleb and I try to keep that on the down low."

She paused suddenly, a hand flying to her mouth as her cheeks flushed bright red. I bit back a smile at the horror flashing through her mind that she had accidentally outed Caleb as a shifter. Catching her eyes, I compelled her to relax as I lifted her hand and bowed over it, pressing a kiss to her knuckles before glancing up at her with my most charming smile. "Have no fear, milady. Your secret is safe with me."

Her cheeks grew even redder as she giggled, but then she paused and looked miserable as though she felt guilty for having a moment of pleasure while her friend was so ill. I carefully closed the door and walked her around to take her seat behind the steering wheel. "Just as every rose has its thorns, even times of sorrow can bring moments of gladness. Please do not feel badly for embracing those moments, Miss

Helena. Now how about you take us to your abode so that I can help you carry Caleb inside?"

It did not surprise me when she immediately agreed; I had compelled her, after all. I flitted around the car and got in on my own side, copying Helena's mannerisms as she fastened the safety contraption across herself—or rather, buckled the belt, as she mentally referred to it. Once we were on the road and I was no longer able to maintain eye contact, Helena seemed to come back to herself a little, as she began giving me the third degree.

"You never did tell me how you so suddenly appeared beside me on that stage back there. Were you there for the program, or do you work for Diane? What part of town do you live in? I'd hate for you to have to walk very far once we reach my house. I'd offer to drive you home but I don't dare leave Caleb alone."

I turned to flash her a charming grin, catching her eye long enough to send a zap of compulsion as I spoke. "No, I do not work there. I have recently arrived in town, on this very day in fact, so I neither have a job nor lodging. Saying that, it occurs to me that I might have a possible solution that would be beneficial to us both. I am thinking you need my help with Caleb, yes? Why not kill two birds with one stone? I seem to be in need of a place to stay, while you lack muscle power to carry our wee wolf back there."

She automatically responded to the compulsion, speaking almost absently. "You need a place to stay and we need help." After she looked away, Helena paused and chewed her lip worriedly before glancing back in my direction. "As tempting as that is, Tobias—I can't really afford to pay an assistant as much as we do need one. Trust me, I've definitely considered the option but the funds just aren't there."

I waved a hand, having no interest in this human's gold. "I am not requesting anything more than room and board. Give me a place to lay my head and a little food in my belly, and I am all yours. Well, Caleb's actually, since he is the one who needs me." *Especially since he is my mate and there is no way I would be leaving his side now that I know of his illness—not that I would have been able to pry myself away from him anyway.*

She started to nod, then began chewing her lip again. I reached out with my magic, easily reading her mind to see her fear about letting a complete stranger under her roof. I waited until she glanced my way again, then sent another compulsory vibe her way.

"I feel as though I owe you an apology because I failed to introduce myself to you properly back at that place. You asked why I was there? I believe we may share a mutual friend who told me you would be there today. She suggested that seeing Caleb in action was not to be missed."

I could practically see the wheels turning in her mind as she tried to decide which friend we might know. As her mind rifled through the names of people, I plucked one out at random. "Heather Gleason, I believe you know her?"

She paused for a moment, then threw her head back with a musical laugh. "Oh, that gossipy little thing? I haven't thought of her in ages! She must follow me on Facebook, I can't think of any other way she'd have known what I was up to these days, let alone where I'd be. My goodness, that takes me back. I haven't seen her since college; when she joined the sorority and I dropped out, but that's a story for another day."

She chattered on about this Heather person that we both supposedly knew, until she abruptly pulled into the driveway of a plain, square home in what appeared to be a quiet neighborhood. The buildings all looked pretty much the same, the only differences were whether the houses were painted gray, tan, or sage green. I had honestly forgotten how bland the human world was, compared to mine.

I pushed aside thoughts of home, focusing instead on the here and now. There was no point in feeling homesick for a realm I would be seeing again in thirty days' time. But even if I never stepped foot on Faelands again, it would be worth it to hear just another few moments of my mate's heartsong.

After I had carefully retrieved Caleb's limp body from the back, I followed her into the house and was relieved to detect a faint bit of his heartsong coming back. Whatever she did outside to make her house blend in with its surroundings, the interior caught me by surprise. I could feel the majicks of Helena's herbs and crystals as I walked in the door. Apparently, my mate's friend was a witch of sorts. I knew it was her because bits of her aura hovered over everything.

I made a mental note to take care around her now that I knew that, wondering why I had not seen it in her mind—yet not at all surprised that she had been so easy to compel. Magical ability or not, she was still a simple human. It troubled me that we had not yet made an accord as to my staying, but I would see that it came to pass. Just another hurdle to cross. First though, I would tend to my mate.

"Lay him down on the soft rug in front of the hearth, Tobias. I'm going to gather some herbs to burn in the fireplace and retrieve my healing crystals. We'll have him awake and perking up in no time." She was already turning to leave as she spoke.

Once she had left the room, I decided to work my own magic and sent a rejuvenating spark, with a touch of my hand along his spine. Caleb opened his eyes, then began to twitch as he seamlessly shifted in a whirl of tooth and claw, flesh and fur, until the wolf became a man again.

A very good-looking man with the same whiskey brown eyes the wolf had. His white-blond hair was startling against his tanned skin, but he was no less beautiful than his wolf had been. He stared at me blankly for several heartbeats until his eyes lit with curiosity. "Who are you and how did I get here? And most importantly, did I manage to check everybody who came to be diagnosed?"

I helped him up and onto the couch, ignoring his questions until I had him settled with a blanket over his lap. I reached to the table beside me, waving a hand just out of his line of sight to produce an earthenware bowl filled with a vegetable soup that would provide the sustenance his body so badly needed. I knelt in front of him, holding out a spoonful of soup for him to take, while I attempted to explain my presence.

"I am Tobias Coppersmith, and your friend Helena has kindly agreed to offer me room and board in exchange for helping you back and forth to your..." My voice trailed off as I tried to think of the word for what he did.

Caleb took the bite of soup, his eyes fluttering shut as if he really enjoyed the flavor. When he opened them again, he reached for the bowl to feed himself, as he supplied the word I had been searching for. "Oh, the seminars? That's a great idea. I hate worrying about whether or not Helena will be stuck with my limp butt if I pass out at one of the seminars, like I apparently did today. I'm assuming I have you to thank for the fact that I made it home in one piece? Poor Helena. The last time it happened, she had to get a couple stagehands to cart my butt to the car, and then she had to leave me there until I woke up. This is a much better way to wake up, so thank you for that."

I could not help but smile at the pleasant, natural way he interacted with me already. Could he hear the heartsong? Or was he just normally this easy to know? We chatted a little more, and I filled him in with more details of my fictional arrangement with Helena, while also making a mental note to myself to compel her later to believe that we had such an arrangement in place.

Once he had finished eating, I took the bowl and pretended to set it aside while I instead majicked it away. No sooner had the bowl disappeared than Helena came bustling back into the room with a bowl of herbs and a mug of tea.

"Oh good, you've met Tobias. I hope he didn't frighten you by the sudden shift to his human form. His body does that on its own when he's recovering from one of his spells. And more importantly, welcome back to the land of the living, Sleeping Beauty! You've got to quit scaring me like that, hon. Here, drink some tea and then we'll see about getting some food into you." She bustled around, focusing on the fire and throwing different herbs onto the flames.

"What do you mean? I'm totally stuffed after that delicious soup. I'm trying to figure out what that one herb was, it was both sweet and savory. Gosh, how long was I out that you had time to make—"

"Oh, look. There is chicory in this tea. How marvelous. You should definitely drink this right down, Caleb. Helena knows what she is doing with her herbs, eh?" I quickly interrupted him, changing the subject to the tea before he could say any more about the soup that Helena definitely had not made. Especially since the sunfresh herb was not one that could be found in this realm.

Helena had not missed the soup comment though, as she looked up from the fire, turning to look at Caleb with a confused frown. I quickly sent her a spark of compulsion as I spoke in a rush. "Now that we have got Caleb up and feeling a bit better, we should take a moment to tell him about our agreement."

Helena frowned thoughtfully as she met my eye. "Our agreement?"

I threw my head back with a laugh, pretending like she was joking, before catching her eye again and holding her firmly in my thrall as I outlined the supposed agreement for

Caleb's benefit. "You are such a tease, Helena, old girl. Now tell Caleb the truth. You have agreed to let me stay here and assist you both in any way necessary, in exchange for food in my belly and a place to lay my head."

Just to solidify it a little more, I reminded her of the mutual friend we were meant to have. "And maybe later you can tell Caleb about our friend, Heather, and some of the hijinks you ladies got up to back in the day."

"Oh, yes." Helena immediately brightened with a smile at Caleb. "I don't believe I've ever told you about Heather, have I? I knew her during that short time I tried the sorority life while you were taking a semester off. Tobias, here, knows her, the poor guy. There's never been a more entitled brat to walk the earth, but bless her heart if she isn't just the sweetest thing. She means well, you know? But she just can't help that snooty little attitude that creeps in. It's not her fault, really. It's all in the upbringing, you know?"

As Helena chattered, I quietly eased onto the couch beside Caleb. Subtly taking my place at his side, while I forced myself to remain patient. While I would find every loophole possible to get Helena working toward my goal, there was no way I would risk things by pushing too fast with Caleb.

Since I couldn't compel him to believe me, or use any majicks to make him fall in love with me, I would just have to be as charming and adorable as possible. They had given me thirty days to win him over, but I had a sick feeling in the pit of my stomach that Caleb simply did not have that kind of time. It was time to turn on the charm.

CALEB

"You're ridiculous," I sputtered as I watched Tobias fill a freaking fanny pack with dog treats. He also had a portable, collapsible water dish that had made its way into the pack. I leaned against the kitchen counter, crossing my arms over my chest as I watched him work. "You do realize that I'm not an actual dog, right? And you aren't taking me for a walk or a run at the dog park? I'm not sure if I should be touched by your concern or completely insulted right now."

Tobias shot me a wink, his mouth curving into that silly slanted smile that never failed to charm me. "Aye, of course you are not a dog, mate. But you are playing one for the crowd, are you not? And these are not normal dog treats. These are bits of homemade beef jerky that were marinated in Helena's healing herbs. The idea is to keep your strength up so that maybe you will not run yourself into the ground again."

By the gods, but it was hard not to crush on this man. And even though I knew he called me *mate* in the easy way people did in the United Kingdom, it still sent a secret thrill through my chest every time I heard it drop from those bow-shaped lips. As sexy as he was though, I'd spent every bit of the past two weeks fighting my attraction.

How could I do otherwise? I had nothing to offer the man, given the fact that my life expectancy had already run past its expiration date. I bit back a sigh. Sexy or not, I had to resist. I'd been inclined to help him find another job and free myself of the temptation he offered... and the willful desire to have more... to have what I could never have in this lifetime.

But I wasn't stupid enough to send him packing, when I'd found myself coming to lean on his strong shoulders, despite my better judgement. Even if Helena would've allowed it, which she never would. Tobias had proven himself to be entirely too helpful at the past three Healing Touch seminars I'd worked. Each time, I'd collapsed on the stage afterward, only to wake up at home feeling refreshed while Tobias fussed over me.

I couldn't say whether it was his attentions or the savory soup that he somehow managed to whip up every time, but I'd been feeling so much stronger since he'd been around. I couldn't put my finger on it, but I just felt more settled around Tobias. Between the peaceful feeling he gave me and his sexy charm, I would've been dropping on all fours and presenting myself for his pleasure, if it weren't for the whole *I'm about to die* thing. Yeah, that wouldn't be fair to him.

"Please do not think I am saying this because I want to see you naked, but should you not be stripping down and shifting soon? We are due at the convention center in twenty minutes, unless I have read your clock wrong." Tobias zipped his fanny pack and gave it a pat. The old-fashioned accessory should've looked ridiculous on him, but as with everything else I'd seen on his body—he somehow managed to rock the look.

I licked my lips as I turned to pull off my shirt. Surely it wasn't normal to be jealous of a fanny pack, right? *And yet...* I sure wouldn't mind being the one to be wrapped around those narrow hips. With my hands locked around and resting over his perky ass... I bit back a groan as I quickly stripped and pushed into my shift. This was definitely not the time to get a boner. All thoughts of an erection, thankfully, dissipated as my body tingled and stretched and reshaped itself into my wolf.

Once I was standing on four paws instead of two legs, I left the kitchen and went to sit by the front door. I wanted to get this over with while I was still feeling the strength I'd drawn from Tobias's presence. I cocked my head to the side, one ear lifting as I tried, yet again, to discern where that wonderful music was coming from. There were times when I could swear it came from Tobias, but that was just crazy. The man seemed almost magical, but he was just a man... not a music box.

"Oh, good. You're ready to go. How are you feeling, hon? You look good. Your eyes have a little sparkle to them today. Should I put your bandanna on here instead of at the venue? Probably not. I know you like it on as little as possible." As usual, Helena was chattering away as if I could answer her in this form.

She'd always treated me that way when I was shifted, ever since we'd met in high school and she'd been the only human I'd trusted with my secret. We'd been assigned to the same foster home and had become fast friends after we'd realized that not only were we both orphans—we were also both queer kids who needed to stick together.

It wasn't so much out of the norm among other shifters for an omega like me to prefer men, but I was a city boy who'd grown up among humans after my parents had died when I was ten and no packs had stepped forward to take in the pup of a pair

SUSI HAWKE

of lone wolves. And let's just say that it doesn't pay to be different when you're a teenager in a human high school. Once we'd befriended each other, Helena and I had been inseparable. After we'd aged out of the system, we'd been roommates ever since.

Helena was rubbing my cheeks, so I pressed my face against her hand in a sign of affection. The hardest part about knowing I was dying wasn't the fact that I'd never meet the love of my life or have a family of my own or any kind of future, actually—no, the hardest part was knowing that I'd be leaving Helena on her own. She must have read something in my eyes because Helena blinked back tears and tapped me on the nose.

"No fair, don't be getting all maudlin on me today. It's bad enough that we have to go off and tell people that they have cancer, I don't need you to be worrying about me too. Pull it together, furface." She scratched under my chin while she blinked rapidly through watery eyes. "I mean it, I can see the sadness written all over your aura. Don't make me pull out a newspaper, I will swat your nose like a bad puppy. Don't make do it, Caley."

Caley. I chuffed at the old, rarely used nickname and twisted my chin around so I could lick her palm. Helena's nose wrinkled as she scrubbed her hand against her hip. "Eww! Doggy slobber, really? Now I really am going to get a newspaper. They still sell those, right? Hmm. I'm going to put an alert on my phone to remind me to look into that."

Tobias's musical chuckle had us both turning to watch him as he walked into the room. "The two of you are a sight to behold, are you not? Shall we be on our way then?"

Helena straightened and reached for her bag. "We shall. The sooner we get there, the sooner we can be headed back home so Caleb can get some rest."

As she opened the door, I rushed past her and let the arid

wind warm my chilled bones as I tuned out the rest of her words. I didn't need to remember how much my calling took out of me. Like I told myself every time we headed for a Healing Touch seminar—if I could save just one person, it would mean my life had meant something.

Today's seminar went more smoothly than any I'd worked in the past few months. Even better? I didn't lose consciousness at the end. Whether it was that comforting music, Tobias's peaceful presence, or the jerky treats and drinks of water that he'd insisted I have between sniffing people, I couldn't say.

Heck, maybe it was a combination of everything. But all I knew as I lay there on my back with my paws in the air after the last person had been evaluated was how much I loved tummy rubs.

I racked my brain, trying to remember if I'd ever let anybody rub my belly before while I was in wolf form, but if I had—I couldn't remember. Either everyone else paled next to Tobias, or I was letting him get closer than anybody ever had. *Whatever.* I wasn't going to lay there and try to figure it out. Nope. I was just going to enjoy the awesome belly rubs while I could. As I could attest, life was too short to do otherwise.

"Let us get out of the house tonight, mate. I promise it is not the dog park I have in mind. What do you say we pack a picnic and go sit on the grass while we partake of our evening meal? We can watch the sunset together. I have heard these kinds of things are good for the soul." Tobias leaned against the kitchen doorway as he spoke, his eyes studying my face as if he were evaluating my current strength level. By the gods, I hated that my friends felt like they had to do that with me.

"Now see, you might have gotten a little more interest if you'd offered the dog park," I said with a laugh. "While I can say no, my wolf is a little whore who's easily bought by those belly rubs you give him."

Tobias made a show of scanning my body while running his tongue over his lips. "Perhaps it is you that should be enjoying the belly rubs, aye? Say the word and I shall rub your belly in every form, mate."

I coughed to cover the blush I felt hitting my cheeks. "Do lines like that really work for you, Tobias? Find someone else to hit on, bud. I'm a bad gamble. And take it from me, when a Las Vegas native tells you something is a poor bet—you should always listen."

Tobias winked smoothly, something I'd never been able to master without looking like I had something caught in my eye. "Sure and should I not be deciding what is a fair bet or not? The truth of the matter is that I have always been a sucker for the underdog—no pun intended, little wolf." When he winked again, it did funny things to my stomach and made me feel all squishy inside.

When I started to decline again, he brought his hand out from behind his back and held out a picnic basket. He stuck out his bottom lip and made the best puppy dog eyes I've ever seen. When I started giggling, his pout turned into a grin as he walked over and held out a hand to pull me from the couch.

"Admit it, mate. You are no match for my charms."

Shit. He wasn't wrong. I looked up at the ceiling as though searching for answers from a higher power before meeting his eyes. "You're really not going to take no for an answer, are you?"

"Why would I be doing that? It is a beautiful day outside,

32

the sunset is fast approaching, and I have readied a beautiful meal that will put some color in your cheeks and bring a sparkle to your eyes." He pulled me smoothly to my feet, holding the picnic basket up to my face as if to tempt me with the delicious aromas emanating from within.

"Dammit. I smell that sweet, savory herb that you refuse to name. Are you sure that thing's not addictive? Because I think I'm getting hooked on it." I frowned at the basket, even while I was leaning closer to get a better whiff.

The rhythm of the mystery music sped up, making me want to dance a jig as Tobias squeezed the hand I'd forgotten he was holding. I found myself laughing and caught up in conversation as he led me out the door and down the street. We were halfway to the park before I realized that he'd gotten his way.

I frowned as the sound of the music roared through my ears, practically vibrating within every cell of my body. Shit, I sure hoped it didn't mean angels were coming for me soon. Was that a thing? Maybe people who were marked for death could hear the heavenly harps in advance? No, that couldn't be it. While there was a bit of plucking strings to the sound, there was also a staccato rhythm that sounded like a drum-beat. Or was it maybe a heartbeat?

I'm not sure what made me do it, but I took a step closer to Tobias and noticed the music grew stronger. When I weaved back over toward the edge of the sidewalk, the music dimmed a notch or two. I tested it out a few more times until I figured I'd proved my hypothesis. Somehow or other, this music was linked to Tobias.

How had I missed that? Wait. I glanced at him out of the corner of my eye, noting his almost ethereal beauty and a sense of something almost otherworldly about him. *Could it be possible…* I mean, surely Tobias wasn't the Angel of Death, right? And if so, was it weird that he turned me on?

I was so lost in my thoughts, that I barely realized it when we arrived at the park. Tobias plucked a blanket out of the basket, spreading it on the ground before taking a seat and tugging me down to sit beside him.

As he pulled out container after container of food, my mind boggled at the impossibility of it all. If I hadn't seen it with my own eyes, I'd never have believed that he pulled such a high volume of items out of such a small basket. The man must have serious Tetris skills, because that was some next level packing.

Tobias kept up an easy conversation, but I was only half listening. I was still toying with the idea of him maybe being an angel of death—was that even a thing? I'd just about decided I was crazy, when a glimmer of something caught the corner of my eye in that magical moment where the sun was setting and the world seemed cast in silver for a split second. I could've sworn I'd seen the flutter of a gossamer rainbow-tinted wing and a flash of a lavender glow, spark in his blue eyes.

This meant one of two things. Either he really was an angel who would be escorting me to the next world in the not-too-distant future, or the brain tumor was affecting me and this was a new symptom. Either way, I threw caution to the wind when I turned to find him watching me. It was as if our lips were magnets and sheer force was pulling them together—I couldn't have fought the kiss if I'd wanted to and I definitely didn't.

As Tobias's lips gently brushed over mine in an almost worshipful caress, the music turned into a crashing crescendo that took my breath away. I gasped against his lips, not sure whether I was still seated on the earth or floating in another reality as the rest of the world faded away and it was just the two of us in this moment. Neither of us tried to deepen the kiss; the moment was almost too reverent for that. Instead, we slowly pulled away, blinking at each other in surprise.

I'm not sure what I would've said—if anything at all—because words probably would have failed me in that moment. So when Tobias flashed me a wink and reached for a container of perfectly made finger sandwiches, I found myself laughing from the absurdity of my life as he held one up to my mouth. "Have a bite, mate. The secret ingredient is that special herb you love so much."

I took a bite of the sandwich, leaving my hands in my lap and letting him feed me. I'd never acted like this in my life, but there was something so precious about the simple act of taking food from his hand that I couldn't resist stealing this one moment of pure joy for myself. After I swallowed, I looked over at him before taking another bite. "You ever going to tell me the name of that herb you're working so hard to get me addicted to? I'm pretty sure I should know the name of my gateway drug, don't you?"

Tobias threw his head back with that musical laugh of his. "Sure, this herb is a gateway to all sorts of bad things. Before you know it, you will be craving rosemary and thyme, maybe even a little mint. Do not worry, mate. I promise I will stop you before I let you get so far as pink peppercorns."

My eyes were wide as I nodded. "Thank you, that means a lot. Everyone knows that pink peppercorns are a hard monkey to get off your back." We shared a smile and I let him feed me another bite before I pressed some more. "Seriously, what's the name of the herb? Helena has been exposing me to everything herbal for the past ten years. You can't live with a Wiccan and not know your herbs. And yet, this one is like nothing I've ever experienced before."

A strange look flashed through his eyes. "Let me just say it is from my homeland and leave it at that. It is not something that Helena would be able to find here anyway, so how about you just let me spoil you and allow me my secrets?"

I studied him for a moment before relenting. "I'm not sure why I have the feeling that you would tell me if you could, or why something like an herb would be a secret in the first place—but I'll back off and let you have your bits of mystery."

Tobias flashed me another one of his smooth winks. "Probably for the best, mate. They say a little mystery is good in a relationship."

I smiled sadly at that one. "Yes, but I wouldn't call one kiss and a couple weeks of friendship a relationship. Besides, I've already warned you—I'm a bad bet, remember? The milk jug in our refrigerator probably has a longer shelf life than I do."

Tobias didn't answer, he simply slid an arm around my shoulders and gently hugged me against his side. Whether he was denying my impending death, or telling me it didn't matter, I accepted the comfort of his hug and decided not to push the point.

A few hours later, Helena and I were enjoying a cup of tea at the kitchen table while Tobias took a shower. Both of us were amused by how much joy he found by the hot running water. It was as if the man had never seen a shower before. Helena's best guess was that he probably hadn't. She cited pictures she'd seen online from homes around the UK with nothing but smallish looking bathtubs and claiming that perhaps our big American showers were a novelty for him.

We weren't exactly sure where he was from, and Tobias was vague when asked, but his accent was too posh and old-world for him to be from anywhere else. At least, that was Helena's contention.

I was pretty sure that Helena was completely wrong on

the bathroom thing, but I wasn't going to argue with her about something so silly when my time was so short. Instead, I preferred to save our arguments for the important things. You know, stuff like whether she or I had the rounder ass—spoiler alert, I totally had a better bubble butt—and which one of us had eaten the last Double Stuf Oreo. Again, I was the guilty party in the Oreo incident. Which oddly enough, could also be the reason why I was the winner of the bubble butt debate as well.

"Sit your skinny little butt back down. Where do you think you're going with that teacup? You know I want to read the leaves, dork." Helena huffed and held out a hand for the cup I'd been about to rinse.

I rolled my eyes as I handed it to her before sitting back down. "Seriously? Are you still trying to win the bubble butt debate? My butt is far from skinny, thank you very much."

Helena snorted, shaking her head as she scanned the leaves in the bottom of my cup. "Only a man would be offended by being told he had a small ass. I guess I don't need to wonder whether you pitch or catch. *Cough*—power bottom—*cough*."

"How many times do I have to tell you that it doesn't work that way with shifters? Keep your human stereotypes to yourself, woman. I'm an omega, so of course I'm a power bottom. Duh." I leaned sideways in the chair to smack my own ass. "Thus, the pride in this prime rump roast. My milkshake brings all the boys to the yard."

We were both fighting a straight face until I said that last bit. It took a few minutes for us to quit laughing long enough for Helena to actually read the leaves. I was expecting her to give me her usual spiel about the leaves saying it wasn't my time yet and they still had plans for me, yada yada yada.

I was pretty sure most of her pep talks were based on her own desires, and not anything she was reading from the leaves, but I'd never called her out on it. I loved that Helena had been at my side throughout my illness, laughing in the face of death with me and encouraging me to stay strong.

Her face sobered as she thoughtfully read the leaves. I'm not sure what it was, but the moment felt so intense that goosebumps raised along my arms. "Come on, Hells. Tell me what you see because you're starting to creep me out."

Helena shook her head. "No, it's nothing like that." She set the cup down and reached for my hands, giving them a squeeze as her eyes lit with the first spark of real hope I'd seen in a long time. "I'm not gonna lie, I have seen death in your leaves before... I just..." Her voice trailed off as she shook her head with a slight frown before looking back at me with pure love shining from her steely gray eyes. "I may have fudged the details in the past, but not this time. Caleb, hon, you've got to believe me when I say there's hope."

When she grew silent again, I squeezed her hands and gave her arms a quick shake. "So are you going to spit it out at some point or make me sit here all night and try to guess? I don't think you want me playing twenty questions, we both know my mind can go into some dark places."

"No kidding, who but you would have guessed that the child would be born with six fingers and webbed toes when people were trying to guess what Cameron's baby would be? Do you have any idea how offensive and fucked up that was to worry an expectant mother?" Helena shook her head at a baby shower gaffe I'd made a few years ago.

I hadn't meant for the slip of paper I'd written that awful guess on to make it into the guessing bowl—and I nearly died of shame when the mother-to-be had read it aloud. It was no excuse, but I'd been in a weird mood and was trying to yank Helena's chain because she'd made me go to Cammie's shower in the first place. Let's just say that was the last time I pulled an asshole joke like that.

"Focus, Helena, Cammie forgave me after her daughter was born healthy, remember? Surely we can let it go and move on, now that the kid is in kindergarten?" I gave her hands another tug.

Helena blew out a breath. "Sorry, I'm deflecting again. I was going over the nuances of the leaves in my mind, trying to make sure I hadn't missed anything before I get your hopes up."

"Hells, I love you like a sister but if you don't just spit it out, I'm going to shift into my wolf and go rub my back on that lovely new navy blue duvet you've got on your bed. You'll still be picking white hairs out of it come Labor Day."

Helena clucked her tongue against the roof of her mouth. "You have such a sweet face for such an evil little man. Remind me why we're friends again?"

"Because you adore me and I complete you in ways that you never knew were possible. Now spill, before I have to follow through on my threat." I flashed her a wink and Helena couldn't help but giggle.

"Don't do that, hon. If anybody but me saw it, they would think you were having a seizure. We've been over this, Caleb. Your eyes were not made for winking." She paused her teasing and gave a nod as if deciding it was okay to finally tell me what she'd seen in my leaves.

Helena gave my hands another squeeze. "Remember, the future is always in flux and the leaves only are a guide of what may be. So here's the thing. For the first time in months, I don't see certain death. Your leaves were filled with crossroads and possibilities. A big decision is looming over you. There's a choice you'll need to make in the near future that will be life-changing. If you choose the option offered, you will have a family and home of your own."

I snorted at that because we both knew damn well that ship had sailed long ago. At twenty-eight years old, it was a

39

sad truth that having a family was never going to be an option for me. There wasn't a chance on earth of that happening. Not after Tina Tumor had taken up residence in my brain.

Helena frowned, jerking my hands this time as she scolded me. "I'm only telling you what I saw in your leaves, jerkface. Who knows what your future holds? You only have to believe the death sentence the doctors gave you, if you are afraid to have faith. But as I said, there's a crossroads in your near future. On the one hand is a family and the home you've always wanted—but on the other is death. This intrigues me, because this is the first that we've seen you having another option besides a one-way ride to the mortuary."

Yeah, I'm not ready to drink that Kool-Aid. I smiled wistfully as I shook my head. "So, about that first path... I have questions. For example, will there be chocolate?"

"No joking, not right now. I'm being serious, hon. If you take the fork in the road that destiny is offering you, our paths will diverge. You won't be part of my life anymore, but you will be alive and that alone will be enough to bring me joy." She blinked back tears and gave my hands another squeeze as she added a thought in a husky voice. "I guess whichever path you take will remove you from my life, won't it? But, Caley... I sure hope you take the path that lets me know you're living your best life happily apart from me rather than the one where I have to visit a cold grave and leave gaudy flowers that we both know you'd hate."

I couldn't take it anymore, I leaned forward and kissed her forehead as I stood and released her hands. "I'll think about everything you said, Hells. But right now, I think I need some fresh air. I'm going to go for a little walk."

She nodded quietly and went back to reading the leaves while I slipped out the back door, intending to use the path from our backyard that would lead me uphill to a portion of unsettled desert where I could let my wolf enjoy a touch of nature. I was surprised when I bumped into Tobias on the back porch. "How did you get out here? I thought you were taking a shower."

He smiled and gave his head a shake—a stray drop of water landing on my cheek where he hadn't dried his hair properly. "I finished about ten minutes ago, but I did not want to intrude on that moment you were having with Helena. May I walk with you?" He smiled gently and offered his arm. Without hesitation, I slipped my hand around his arm and led him toward the back gate.

We walked in companionable silence as I led him to my favorite little oasis at the top of the small hill behind our house. Surrounded by cacti and pebbled sand, we could stand there with our feet firmly entrenched in the beauty of the natural world while gazing down at the glittering lights of the city spread out below us and feast our eyes on the equal magnificence of the man-made world.

As we stood there, Tobias slipped behind me, his arms sliding around my waist as he bent slightly to rest his chin on my shoulder. Our height difference wasn't more than a few inches, but it was just enough that I felt comforted and protected by his embrace.

The now-familiar music that always accompanied his presence spread through my body, filling me with its melodic rhythm while my own heart seemingly supplied the staccato beat. I turned in his arms, wrapping my arms around his waist as I gazed into his moonlit eyes.

The magnetic thing happened again and I was leaning up to kiss him before I realized my intention. This time, the kiss was a little more passionate, although still pretty much PG-rated. His tongue traced my lips, but made no attempt to press inside my mouth. With a final brush of our lips, I leaned back and chuckled nervously.

I blinked a couple times before I found the courage to speak the insanity that had lodged itself inside my mind. "That music I hear. It's you, isn't it?" At his nod, I rushed on. "I knew it. And I think I know why. You're my angel of death, aren't you? You've come to take me to the next world."

Tobias's eyes widened with surprise before he barked out a laugh. "No, mate. Holy shite. Not even close... well, maybe a bit? But no, I have so much more to offer you than death. And trust me, love... I am definitely no angel."

5

TOBIAS

*C*aleb stared at me for a second, his eyes filled with questions that I was not sure I would be able to answer. I looked around and spotted a large rock at the edge of the clearing. Tipping my head toward it, I caught his hand and brought it to my lips for a quick kiss. "Shall we have a seat and share a bit of conversation?"

"Sure, it's a warm night and I'm not in any rush to go home just yet." Caleb sighed gently and wove his fingers through mine as we walked. "I hate to always bring my upcoming death into every conversation, but I don't know how many more nights I have like this, you know? A three-quarter moon, warm desert breezes, and a million or two twinkling stars overhead—what more could a guy ask for, am I right?"

"I can think of many things a guy might ask for, mate. But let me start by asking you for a little conversation." I sat down on the rock, pulling him onto my lap without asking. I wondered for a moment if I had overstepped, but his arm immediately went around my neck as he snuggled up against me, fitting perfectly on my lap.

"What did you want to talk about, Tobias? Are we going to discuss that cryptic comment you made about having more to offer me than death, or the whole part where I accused you of being an angel or some shit?" Caleb stopped to chuckle, shaking his head at his own mistaken belief. "At least I didn't try to call you a Grim Reaper. I've never seen you hold a scythe, and am pretty sure you can't pull off black —although, pretty much any other color works for you. It's really not fair for one man to be so damn pretty."

I shrugged at the compliment. There was no point in arguing the truth, I did have a pretty face. "Is not black the absence of color? Or is it all the colors? I always get confused on that."

"If you were to ask an artist, they'd tell you that black absorbs all the colors equally and reflects nothing back, but scientists consider it the absence of colors but… you know what? Never mind." Caleb started to explain then shook his head. "Sorry. It occurs to me that I don't want to joke around or exchange frivolous factoids. Instead, I feel like I need to make you understand why there can't be anything between us, despite the obvious chemistry we share."

I was definitely going to have to disagree with that notion, but I kept my thoughts to myself for the moment. "All right, how about you tell me what you think I need to know?"

He took a deep breath and stared off into the distance as if admiring the lights of the city. "I know Helena told you about my tumor, but did she tell you that I was given three months to live? There's nothing they can do for me, Tobias. Let me just put that out there so you don't have any misconceptions."

Shite. This was worse than I thought, and I had seen him at his weakest. The only thing that had been bolstering him over the past couple weeks was the occasional sparks of healing majicks I had snuck his way, and the sunfresh herb he so enjoyed. I figured the bits of healing majicks were another loophole, since I had not ever used enough to make it obvious or give myself away. If Easton and his friends had a problem with it, surely they would have put a stop to things by now.

I took a breath and forced myself to remain calm. "And how much do you have left of those three months?"

Caleb smiled sadly. "The three months ended seven weeks ago. When I tell you I'm living on borrowed time, I'm not exaggerating. My expiration date passed and somehow I'm still sitting here. Please don't think this is a pity party, because I am strangely resigned to my fate. This is just me being completely honest with you so that you can understand what I'm facing and why I can't let anything happen between us, no matter how alluring I find you."

I considered that for a few moments and reached up to cup his chin, gently turning his face toward mine as I leaned in to kiss those tempting lips. His lips parted on a sigh as I broke the kiss and leaned back again. I stroked his cheek with my thumb while I reached deep within myself for the courage to ask him to give me a shot.

"Listen, mate. I hear what you are saying and I understand that you are trying to protect my heart. How about this... what if you took a cancer break for tonight and pretended that we are just a couple. We can be two men who met on vacation and fell in love at first sight. If that were the case, what would you want to do right now?"

Caleb looked like he wanted to promise me the moon for a moment, then his eyes shuttered as he shook his head. "That's a nice fantasy, but it's not fair to you. I won't lie and say that I don't believe we could have meant so much to each other had we met under different circumstances. But I'm not going to leave you grieving when I move on from this world."

I waited for him to collect himself enough to look me in

45

the eye again. Once I had his attention, I leaned forward and brushed my lips over his again before I spoke. "That is my decision to make, is it not? Instead of worrying about leaving me to grieve, why not ask me this instead: ask me if I might rather have one night in your arms and know that I brought you happiness or to turn and walk away, never to have known the taste of your skin."

Caleb's eyes glazed over as a soft smile curved his lips. "Dammit, you and those lines. I swear, you could charm anyone if you put your mind to it, couldn't you?"

I tipped my head to the side with a slight shrug. "The concept is not entirely impossible, no. So tell me, mate—was that a yes or a no to that one night in your arms?"

He started to shake his head then stopped, his shoulders releasing the slightest bit of tension as he leaned forward to rest his forehead against mine. "You win, I can't resist an offer like that. But you're probably going to have to carry me home because you've left me a little weak in the knees."

Before he had a chance to change his mind, I was on my feet and cradling him in my arms as I walked as fast as this human version of myself would allow. Caleb's laughter sounded like joyful giggles that trailed behind us, lighting the darkness with his special brand of light. When we got back to the house, I knew the moment I opened the door that it was empty. I wondered where Helena was but Caleb merely laughed again as I spoke my thought aloud.

"Helena is perceptive, if you haven't noticed. Not to mention the fact that she probably saw something in the leaves. This is her telling us to enjoy a little private time. We won't see her again until tomorrow morning. She's more than likely going to spend the night with one of the members of her circle."

When I carried him into his room, I kicked the door shut behind us before walking over and laying him on the bed.

"Enough about Helena, mate. Since she cleared out to give us our night together, how about we make the most of it, hmm?"

Caleb watched as I pulled off my clothes, his eyes glazed with passion as he took in my naked form. I resisted the urge to preen and pose for my mate. This night was not about boosting my own ego. No, this night was my one chance to make him love me and maybe—just maybe—share love's true kiss that would allow me to tell him what I had to offer with the portal to my realm.

After I set my clothes aside, I turned to help Caleb undress, but he had already kicked off his clothes and was stretched on the bed watching me through hooded eyes as he stroked his own cock.

I laid down beside him, stretching out on my side and pushing his hand away to replace it with my own. He caught my eye with a determined look on his face. "Do me a favor? Just remember what you said back there about us just being a pair of normal guys and don't treat me like glass, okay? I'm not fragile."

My voice was thick with emotion as I spoke. "I know, mate. You are about the strongest man I have ever met." As I stroked his length, I bent to cover his lips with mine. Caleb thrust into my hand, trying to push things along and rush us to the next step, but that was not my plan.

After one more firm stroke, I released his cock and ran my hand down his leg and back up his inner thigh. Ignoring his most obvious erogenous zones, I lazily traced along every crease and dip as if mapping out a mental picture of his body through touch.

Until now, I had purposely kept our kisses chaste but now that we were in his bed, I did not resist as Caleb's tongue tentatively pressed against the seam of my lips. I tilted my head, opening my mouth to let him in as I rolled over on top of him.

Our heartsong throbbed between us, forming an entirely new rhythm as our bodies rubbed against each other while we kissed. I poured every bit of the passion and desire I felt into that kiss and was pleased to feel the same come back from Caleb through the song. Where the melody had been almost haunting and compelling, now it was joyous. It was as if our hearts were singing to each other with every beat.

I ran my hand along his side, pausing to cup his perky butt cheek in my palm and give it a promising squeeze before sliding my hand along the back of his thigh as I lifted and guided it to curve over my waist. His other leg moved of its own accord, his ankles locking over my arse as a sweet new smell wafted through the air.

I broke our kiss, sniffing to discover the source of this heady scent. It was as if daffodils had been mixed with the fragrance of a spring rain. Caleb stared at me in wonder, "What do you smell? Surely you can't smell the true essence of my slick?"

Rather than seem like an idiot and ask what he meant, I gently tapped his mind for the answer. Once I saw what he meant—*slick* being the special lubricant that omegas secrete when aroused—I could not resist sliding my hand between his luscious cheeks and feeling it for myself.

I ran my fingers over his pucker, scooping up a little bit of the slick before bringing my hand back up to my face. Caleb stared at me with fully dilated pupils as I smelled my finger, closing my eyes as I inhaled deeply of his essence. When I opened my eyes again, I locked my gaze on his as I licked my finger clean.

"Fuck yessss," Caleb said on a moan. I smiled and bent to kiss him again while my hand migrated back to that slick little hole. Caleb was writhing beneath me, our cocks sliding together deliciously while I worked him open with a finger. My mate reached between us, taking our cocks together in his hand as he gave them a few strokes, letting the liquid dripping from our slits act as a lubricant to ease his way.

"That's interesting, have you noticed we're the same exact size?" He panted out his words between strokes.

I smiled at that, thinking of the surprise coming his way. "Are we now? Imagine that."

His hand fell away as I slid him higher in the bed and pushed the head of my cock against his entrance. "Are you ready for me, mate?"

Caleb groaned and rocked his hips against me. "Past ready. Hurry up and get in there before I change my mind."

I grinned at his sass and pressed into his slick heat. His walls were a snug fit, but I knew I would be expanding them soon enough. Caleb's legs loosened their hold around me and he dropped them to the sides as if offering better access. When his body was completely relaxed, I carefully began to thrust.

Time lost all meaning as our heartsong washed over us, filling the room with its unique melody. Between that and the fragrance of his slick, I was ready to cry out my love for him as my heart beat with his name. Thump-thump. Ca-leb. Thump-thump. Ca-leb. Our hips rocked in rhythm with the heartsong. It was as though we were both finely attuned to its beat and our bodies naturally fell into harmony to complete the tune that only we could make.

Caleb gasped as my cock swelled and thickened within him. He would not know it right now, but it was also lengthening with each thrust. When Caleb tried to speed us along by rocking his hips faster, I simply caressed my hands over his skin and nuzzled his neck to slow him down again. I didn't need to pound into him at a punishing speed; instead, I willed my cock to lengthen that much more and fill him completely as I rocked against him with shallow thrusts.

As the heartsong sped up, I rocked my hips a little faster to match its beat—while still taking care to treasure my mate's body as I worshiped him with mine. I grazed my teeth over the special gland in the crook of his neck, smiling to myself at the way his body trembled at the touch. When his breathing became erratic and his body began to stiffen, I allowed my cock to completely fill his channel and lock us together.

Where his kind had a knot, mine had what we called an energy lock. The life forces between mates worked like magnetic poles and would lock us together using the energy of our passion. I was not sure how long we would remain locked, since this only existed between mates and I had never taken a mate before.

I was so close; my entire body was on fire and I could feel the energy rippling over my skin. Caleb's eyes widened as a lavender glow burst out of my aura and covered us both as one flesh, bathing us in its shining light.

He opened his mouth as if he were going to speak, then completely shocked me by jerking his head forward and plunging elongated fangs into my flesh—just as he would have done if he were claiming an alpha for a mate. I did the only thing I could since my balls were so tight and I knew I was about to explode at any moment—I gave his neck an answering bite and claimed him as mine.

The moment my teeth sank into his skin, the heartsong reached a pounding crescendo and the lavender light pulsed in rhythm with its beats while the fire in my balls shot along my cock and my seed burst forth into his channel. I was vaguely aware of a burning itch along my shoulder blades, but I was too distracted by the sticky heat of my mate's cum spilling between our tightly pressed bodies. My hands cupped his ass as I gave a few final thrusts until I had emptied my balls.

I turned to kiss him after licking a few droplets of blood away from where I had bit, only to be met by his wide-eyed, awestruck gaze. His voice was hushed and reverent as he stared over my shoulders. "Are those... wings? I thought you said you weren't an angel! I don't understand. What's happening, angel?"

I glanced over my shoulder, unsurprised to see my wings had fully unfurled—despite the glamour I had had in place to hide them should they pop out of their own volition. When I turned back to explain, he took a ragged breath and reached up to run a finger over the tips of my ears where their true pointed form was also clearly visible, judging by the fact that he was currently enamored by them. When he finally looked back at me, Caleb's eyes were filled with wonder as he repeated himself. "What's happening, angel?"

Chuckling with relief, I shot him a grin. "I thought I told you I am no angel, mate. As for what is happening? I am pretty sure I have just been given permission to tell you my secret."

6

CALEB

*M*y eyes narrowed as I stared into Tobias's glowing eyes. And where had that lavender glow come from? Well, aside from the one that was sparkling around us like we were in some sort of spotlight. No, that didn't work. The light wasn't so much glowing onto us as it was streaming out from within us. *Yeah, I really needed some answers.*

"What do you mean you've been given permission to share your secret? What's going on here, angel boy?" Even as I spoke, I was looking over his shoulders at those beautiful wings. They were nearly translucent, yet still contained a gorgeous array of color. The very tips were black then faded into jeweled tones of royal blue and turquoise patched together in a mosaic. When the turquoise lightened in the center of his wings, it then mixed with shades of lavender and then back into darker purples and more teal.

They were uniquely gorgeous and absolutely breathtaking. I wanted to reach out and touch them. My finger was already moving before the thought finished processing. As I got close, the wing flinched and flapped a few times like a butterfly leisurely fluttering its wings in the breeze. As soon as I compared it to a butterfly, I pulled my finger back with a gasp. Could I hurt his wing the same way that moths and butterflies could be wounded from a mere touch?

Tobias chuckled, easily following my thoughts by my reaction. "Easy, mate. You can touch them, that was just me teasing you a bit. Go ahead and run your finger along the membrane—you know you want to."

I did. I really, *really* did.

Biting my lip, I stretched my hand out again, ready to run a tentative finger along the line of his wing. Just as I got close again, the wings flapped back and forth a few times. The force of it was enough to send a breeze through the room and lift a loose paper from my dresser. I watched in amazement as the wings flapped a little more, sending the paper floating through the air. When the wings suddenly stilled, the paper fell to the floor.

Tobias threw his head back with a laugh, obviously enjoying his little teasing game. While he was distracted, I reached out and grabbed the edge of his wing. His laughter stopped and he winced as though in pain. I lightened my grip on the wing, but didn't let go. He wasn't going to pull my leg again—that is... if he was teasing. I wasn't sure what to think just yet. I watched as his face lit up with amusement.

"Well done, mate. You have truly caught me now, have you not? And no, that does not hurt me in the slightest." The sincerity in his eyes told me that he spoke the truth.

Breathing a little easier now, I rubbed the pad of my thumb over the soft, almost satiny wing. My voice came out in a whisper, I was too awed for anything more than that. "They are so beautiful, angel boy. It looks as though the membranes should be fragile because they appear so delicate. They look as if they're maybe made of cellophane? No, not cellophane. That's too cheap and crinkly. See-through tissue paper maybe? Still crinkly, but fragile. But no... this is solid to the touch. And so soft! I almost want to rub my face over your wings."

Immediately, the wings fluttered and flapped forward. I jerked my hand back just in time to avoid tugging on it and accidentally hurting him—if that were possible, who knew at this point. *Friggin' tease.*

When Tobias rubbed the tip of his wing over my cheek in a tender caress, I was glad I'd released my grip because the intimate brush of his wing against my cheek was... well, probably the most breathtaking thing I'd ever experienced.

It took me a moment to get over my wonder before my brain fully engaged and I remembered that I still needed answers. I shivered as his wing tickled my hairline and reached up to brush it back over his shoulders with a light giggle.

Seriously, a giggle? Yeah, this man had me so giddy that I was actually giggling.

I fixed my fiercest glare and jutted my chin in his direction. "I believe I was looking for some answers? Enough distraction, Tobias. You need to keep your sexy wings to yourself for a bit. Tell me the truth. Are you an angel or not?"

Tobias shook his head with a solemn expression. "No, I am definitely not angelic. Before I answer, can I just ask why you are so easily able to accept my wings and pointy ears?"

As soon as he mentioned the ears, my gaze shot to the pointed tips. I'd nearly forgotten those! I ran a hand over the shell of his ear and around the curve to the tippy top where it pointed just like I'd expect from an elf or other fairy creature. As soon as that thought flitted through my head, I dropped my hand with a gasp. "You're a fairy!"

Tobias looked almost offended. "I most certainly am not. Fairies are inane, prattling little woodland creatures who flitter and flutter among the flowers and herbs like bees. No, I am Fae."

He spoke so proudly, I had to bite my cheek to keep from laughing. "Isn't that the same thing? I mean..." I waved a hand toward his jeweled wings. "You both have wings, right?"

"And that is the only thing we have in common, mate. If you would not mind circling back to my question though... why does this not disturb you? I would think my truth might be a little unsettling for you."

I snorted out a laugh. "Seriously? Dude. I'm a shifter and my best friend is a witch. Weird is kinda my wheelhouse." I reached up and rubbed my thumbs over the pointy tips of his ears again. "So tell me your secret, Tobias. Or was the whole fairy thing your secret? And who—or what—would've given you permission to tell me?"

"Fae," he corrected absently. "I was brought here through a magical portal from my realm to yours that appeared in my private chambers. What else could I do but cross through and have a peek about? When I arrived, I was met by a group of people, shifters actually."

He paused and took a breath, as if trying to decide how to explain. "There is a whole history that would take more time than we have to properly tell, but I shall sum it up by saying that a millennia or two ago, my people and other immortal beings walked the earth among the humans. A war was fought between the Fae and the gods—with humanity in the crossfire. A group of ancient shamans forged a treaty in blood that was signed by emissaries of both sides with the agreement that we would all return to our own realms, and the portal would be locked behind us."

My heart raced with excitement as my mind began connecting dots. "The legacy families! It was like an urban legend among our people for generations until about twenty-five or thirty years ago, when the legacy families stepped forward and admitted that they existed. They told the story of their ancestors saving the world by sending the immortals away. According to our history, it was those shamans who were the forefathers of the modern day alphas and omegas. They started teaching it to us after the legacy families came forward. Now I don't know the full history, aside from what I've picked up online because I wasn't raised in a pack. My parents weren't part of any packs. They were city wolves who kept to themselves."

Tobias nodded with understanding. "Yes, that is about right from what I know. I do not know what happened to those shamans or their descendants after the portal closed, but a few of the shifter minds I have gleaned information from since I have been back on this plane have that same knowledge of your history that you speak of—more or less."

I studied him for a moment, my mind whirling with questions. "What do you mean by gleaning information? That's a weird expression."

He looked hesitant for a moment then shot me a wry grin. "It is not so much an expression, as the truth. I use my majicks to pull information from the minds of people I pass as I go around town. That is how I was able to fill in the blanks of human history while I was seeking you."

I really wanted to sit up and push him aside so I could hear more about this without being held in his arms... but our bodies were locked together by some weird magic juju. He didn't have a knot, at least not like any I'd ever heard of— and yet, his cock was firmly locked inside my channel so tightly that neither of us were going anywhere anytime soon. I made a note to ask about that later, because I didn't want this conversation to get derailed.

"Why were you seeking me in particular? Can you at least explain that much to me?"

Tobias was leaning on his forearms, but he folded his

wings back without so much as a wink and rolled us over so that I was straddling his body. I wondered where his wings had gone as I wriggled around to get more comfortable, leaning my arms on his chest to rest my chin while we talked.

"That is part of the secret, mate. Do you not hear the music of our heartsong? Listen closely and you will hear the harmony that our hearts make when we are together."

I sucked in a breath as that now familiar music ebbed and flowed around us. If I closed my eyes, I could almost see the music moving through my cells with every heartbeat. "I knew that music was somehow coming from you! How is that possible? That's been *us* this whole time?"

Tobias lifted a hand to cup the back of my neck. He gave it a gentle squeeze, much like any alpha would do. "Remember, I am not human. Unlike you, I do not contain a soul. I am an immortal being. Without a soul, I do not have the same capacity to find a mate as you shifters do. Where you would recognize the other half of your soul through scent or how you feel in each other's presence—my people find their other half this way. I do not have a soulmate; I have the other half of my heartsong. When I am near my perfect mate, the music is heard by both of us. It is every bit as much a special bond as you would have with a soulmate, it is just different. Does that make sense?" His blue eyes bore into mine, searching me as if looking for acceptance. I couldn't help but notice the violet glow that still glowed between us.

I put a hand to the bite mark he'd placed on my neck. "But I didn't feel anything binding us together through your bite." I shook my head as soon as those words came out of my mouth. "No, that's not entirely true—the music has gotten stronger and purer, if that makes sense. But I don't feel completely connected to you like I've always heard happens through the mating bite. I guess I kind of figured we were just caught up in the fantasy, not that we were really bonding."

He shook his head. "It was not a fantasy. You really are my mate. But I do not believe we can be fully bonded until you have made a decision."

I frowned in confusion. "What possible decision could I need to make? I hate to be a wet blanket, but it's not like I'm going to be around long enough to make any life-changing choices at this point."

Tobias smiled gently, wrapping his arms around me as he craned his neck forward to brush a kiss over my forehead. "Aye. How about we sleep on it, Caleb? You might be surprised at the answers that can arise after a good night's sleep. I do not wish to sound cryptic, but I was not given all of the answers. I was told to find you, and an opportunity would be presented."

As he said that, a yawn escaped me and I suddenly realized how completely and utterly exhausted I was. I moved my arms up to slide beneath his head as I rested my cheek against his chest. I didn't know how long this energy lock would work, but I didn't hate how closely connected it made us. "Our answer's going to magically come to us in our sleep? Is that what you're saying?"

"I do not know the answer to that, but I have a strong feeling that we are meant to sleep now. And no, this is nothing I have knowledge of—it is just a gut feeling. Not to mention the fact that a night's rest might help me figure out how to explain things better. I have yet to tell you how I came to arrive here, other than that I crossed through a portal. I was brought here by those legacy shifters you mentioned, along with the missing prince of my realm. At least I solved the mystery of where he has been hiding these many years."

Snuggling deeper against him, I felt the drowsiness really

taking hold. "How about you tell me all about it over break-fast? I think I'm going to sleep now." His answering chuckle was the last thing I heard as sleep pulled me under.

When my eyes opened, I found myself standing in an ancient stone circle. It almost reminded me of Stonehenge, but not quite. The craggy hills surrounding us made me think of a documentary I'd seen about Scotland, or even Outlander, which was really confusing.

It took me a moment before I realized that Tobias was standing beside me, and we were surrounded by a group of strange men. They were all about my age, give or take. As I looked a little closer, I saw their eyes take on distinctive glows. I sucked in a breath as I felt a swirl of energy brush over me, leaving a trail of goosebumps in its wake. I started to reach for Tobias's hand, but a voice stopped me in my tracks.

"No, you can't touch—that's the number one rule of dream walking." I stared in shock as a beautiful twink of mixed ethnicities stepped forward. Despite his abrupt tone, his eyes were filled with kindness—and a faint bronze glow.

When he blinked, the glow disappeared, leaving me to believe that he'd allowed them to shine on purpose. "Hello, Caleb. My name is Oni, and these are members of my pack. We represent the legacy families. We've been tasked to do a job for the goddess Artio." As he spoke, he motioned to the other men who nodded and smiled. A gorgeous alpha who exuded power from every pore stepped up to stand beside Oni. The omega smiled up at the alpha before turning back to me. "This is my mate, Connor. He and his brothers have constructed this dreamscape so we could meet at last."

I finally found my voice, blurting out the first thought

that came through my head when he paused to take a breath. "What the hell is a dreamscape?"

The alpha and his brothers roared with laughter. The three men were obviously triplets, although the brothers appeared to be omegas based on their scents. I started to ask why I could smell them in a dreamscape, but held my tongue when one of the brothers began to speak.

"It's rather disconcerting, isn't it? My name is Samuel, but my friends call me Sammy. A dreamscape is basically a waking dream. Your mind and soul are able to be present with us, while your body sleeps in its bed across the ocean. While you're within the construct, you can use all of your senses—except for touching another living thing. If you touch any of us, the dream ends and you will wake up in your bed."

Oni rubbed his hands together. "Now that we've established that, why don't we explain why you're here?" At my nod, he continued. "We brought your mate from his realm, and gave him thirty days to find the other half of his heartsong. He was told that if he was able to find you and share love's true kiss within thirty days, then we would offer a choice to you both. Tobias didn't know all the details, only that he needed to find you and let you fall in love with him for himself. He wasn't allowed to use spells, majicks or beguilement—which was a challenge for him, I'm sure. The Fae tend to lean heavily on their majicks."

I found myself feeling confused again. "But we haven't said we loved each other? I mean, we've kissed and… other things… but we've never proclaimed our love for each other."

A beautiful man that I hadn't seen before—a golden Adonis with magic exuding from him so powerfully that I knew without seeing any wings or pointy ears that he was the Fae prince Tobias had mentioned—stepped forward with a charming smile. "Aye, but you didn't need to say the words.

61

The emotion was in your heart, or you never would've seen his wings. In the moment of your mating, your heart was filled with such true affection for Tobias which made his concealing majicks fall away. It was because you care for him, that you were able to see past his glamour."

Tobias rocked back-and-forth on his feet, his arms crossed over his chest as he listened. "Ah, so that is how that happened. I thought one of you buggers had done it. So when I shared those things with him, I was not breaking any rules?"

Sammy smiled almost affectionately at Tobias. "Not at all, because love's true kiss had already been exchanged."

Before anyone else could speak, Oni snapped his fingers to get our attention. "They have years of pillow talk awaiting them where they can discuss that, let's get back to the matter at hand, shall we?"

Connor cast an adoring smile at his saucy little mate, shaking his head as he spoke. "Oni is blunt, but he is correct. Time is of the essence, as we all know. So here's what we have to offer you, Caleb. Our goddess has given us permission to choose worthy Fae to cross the portal and find their mates. Once love's true kiss has been shared, you are given the option to stay together. The Fae can exchange his immortality to stay here in our realm where he'd be given a human soul and an average life expectancy. As a boon, the Fae can choose a spirit animal and become a shifter like his mate."

Oni spoke up again. "Or, and this is where you might be interested—the human shifter can trade his soul for immortality and moved to the Fae realm. Understand though, this is a one-way trip. Choose wisely, because if you want to be together then you'll have to choose one realm or the other. We can't have immortals hanging around our world longer than one lunar cycle. Likewise, those with a soul cannot stay long in the Fae world. Once you've given up your soul, you wouldn't be able to stay here either."

My mind was racing as I tried to make sense of what they were saying. "But why would Tobias want to give up his immortality to be with me? I'm not going to be alive much longer anyway."

Before I could explain that any further, Sammy held up a hand. "We are aware of your health issues, Caleb. Pardon us for being intrusive, but we have psychic abilities and are given visions, whether we ask for them or not. There isn't much time left within the lunar cycle, so you need to decide quickly if you would like to return home with Tobias. Yes, you face uncertain death in this realm. But you could save your life and have a mate and an entirely new future if you choose to trade your soul for immortality by going to the Fae realm. The two of you need to return here to us on the night of the full moon with your decision."

"But that's this weekend!" I don't know why this made a difference. These men were offering to save my life, and I was freaking out because I didn't have time to think about it? What the hell was wrong with me?

Tobias turned to look at me, his eyes filled with a mixture of hope and dread. It was as though he were afraid to believe that I might be willing to give up my life here—such as it was —to join him in his world. "What do you think? Would you be interested in coming back to my world? Honeymeade is a welcoming town, and my family would love you."

I stared at him blankly for a moment. I couldn't take in the idea of moving to another realm—let alone having a family—but yet, how could I say no to living? Especially if that life would include having Tobias at my side? *Duh*. No question.

Shaking my head, I said pretty much exactly that. "Seriously? You're asking if I would rather choose to stay here and die, or go there and live forever with you? How is this even a question?"

The one named Sammy chuckled at my tone. "It sounds as though you have a good conversation ahead of you. We'll let you two return home. Just remember, you will need to be here before the moon reaches its apex with your answer." As soon as he spoke, he reached his hands out and clasped each of his brothers'. Just as we'd been warned, the moment their hands touched, I found myself blinking awake back home in my bed.

I looked around in confusion, trying to decide if I'd just dreamed that craziness, or if it were really real. Tobias moved in bed, reaching over to flick on the light before sitting back against the headboard. He held out an arm as if to invite me to snuggle against his side. Although his wings were no longer showing, his pointy ears remained.

Scooting back, I leaned into his embrace and rested my head on his shoulder. "Am I correct in assuming that I didn't just imagine that whole dreamscape thing?"

He chuckled softly, resting his cheek against the top of my head. "Aye. That really happened, mate. Are you ready to talk about the opportunity at hand? Forgive me if I sound selfish, but I do not want to live without you now that I have discovered your existence. This would sound ridiculous if you had not heard our heartsong for yourself, but you are my melody. I would not wish to live a life without you in it—I apologize if that puts too much pressure on you."

Heartsong aside, I knew in my heart that Tobias was my other half. To be given such an amazing opportunity was more than a dream come true—it was a miracle. "Why would I ever say no? All I have waiting for me here is death. I have no family. All I have is—" I sucked in a breath, jerking away to stare at him in horror.

Tobias nodded sadly. "Helena?"

As if hearing her name, there was a knock on the door just before it was flung open and Helena herself came running in. I pulled up the blankets so that we wouldn't give her a show. "Privacy, Hells! Perhaps you've heard of it?" I was only teasing, as she well knew. The thing about being as close as we were, was that there were little to no boundaries left between us.

Proving this to be true, Helena climbed right up on the bed and came to a stop between us, sitting back to curl her legs under herself as she faced us. "I'm sorry, but I was reading the leaves again and then Aubrey had a vision." She started talking so fast that I could barely keep up.

She paused somewhere in the middle of telling us about the psychic dream that her friend had, dissolving into squealing giggles as she flung herself forward and wrapped her arms around both of our necks to pull us into a group hug. "I'm so excited! I don't know how it's going to happen but you're going to live and you're going to embark on a grand adventure!"

I was laughing as I shoved her off me. "You do realize that we're both naked under these blankets, right? You totally just barged in on our pillow talk, brat."

Helena waved a hand. "You'll have plenty of time for that later. And do you know why?" She paused before screaming out her next thought in another wild squeal. "Because you're going to live!"

I held up a hand to stop her. "Hells, there's only one problem—in order for me to live and have this grand adventure? I would never be able to see you again. How can I do it? I would miss you too much. I don't know if I could do that without you."

"Are you kidding me? Don't be daft. I'll miss you too, but this way I can miss you and know that you are safe and happy and out there living your best life somewhere, instead of being, you know... dead."

"But Hells... what if I asked them if you could come too? Would you want that?" I paused for a moment, glancing at Tobias with a worried frown. I hadn't even thought to consult him before making that grand offer. He just smiled and wrapped his arms around me, pulling me back against his chest.

Helena watched us for a moment, then bit her lip as she shook her head. "That's not the road I'm meant to take, Caley. I know my path, and this is where ours diverge. I can't imagine living without you either, but I also can't abandon my circle or the people who rely on me for healing. I wish you well and I will send you off with my blessings, but I must stay here."

A tear streaked down her face, matching the one that was making a track down mine. Tobias kissed the top of my head and loosened his hold on me so he could lean forward. "Helena, would you mind running to get that lovely crystal ball you keep in the front parlor?"

Helena looked disconcerted, but she jumped off the bed and ran off to do as he'd requested. Before I had a chance to ask why in the world we needed her crystal ball, Helena was already coming back in with it in her arms. Tobias reached for it, flashing us both a wink as he stretched his fingertips over the crystal.

Bright blue sparks shot between his hands and the glass. After a few seconds, he reached out for my hand. It felt like a live current was passing over my skin, making the hair on my arms stand on end as he placed my hand over the ball and hovered his directly over top. Warmth spread through my body and red sparks shot from my fingertips, mixing with the blue coming from his other hand.

Tobias lowered his palm to touch my skin. The moment

we connected, our blue and red lights created a purple that went directly into the ball. Helena and I both watched, totally and completely transfixed as a ball of purple light flickered from within the crystal ball. Tobias released my hand before passing it to Helena with a smile.

He turned to flash us both a wink as he leaned back against the headboard again. "I am probably breaking many rules, but this will enable you to check on Caleb and view him twice a year. During the solstice when the veil is thin, your crystal ball will work. You will not be able to speak to him, but you will be able to see him. After you have lived your life, and pass onto the next, the majicks I have imbued into your crystal will end. But until then, I promise you will be able to see him for as long as you live. Now give your friend a hug and tell him you love him—I think you both need that right now."

Helena looked at Tobias with a strange mixture of skepticism and respect—along with her trademark smirk that said she thought he was more than a little bit weird—before she leaned forward and hugged me as he'd suggested, when I leaned forward and held out my arms.

While we hugged, we both said how much we loved each other. I felt the surge of magic around us and heard the snapping of fingers. We pulled apart and turned to see Tobias holding out his hand. In his palm were two crystal hearts with multifaceted prisms.

Tobias winked again. "Go on, take your gifts—I have made one for each of you. Apparently, they have decided to allow me to have my majicks working in full now." Helena and I exchanged excited smiles before reaching for the prisms.

Tobias waited until we each held one before explaining more. "Hold them to the light and watch the wall behind the lamp."

I held mine up and watched in wonder as an image of the two of us hugging played out on the wall and I could clearly hear Helena speak. *"I love you, Caley. I will love you always and forever. Go and live your happiness. Be free and know that I will always carry a piece of you in my heart."* Helena held hers up until dueling images played on the wall while a similar statement from me echoed around the room.

Helena and I exchanged another excited grin before we both tackled Tobias into a big hug. Helena kissed his forehead and each of his cheeks before leaning back and hugging the crystal to her heart. "You are the best man ever, Tobias. Both for loving my Caley, and for giving us this memento to cherish."

When Tobias blushed at her gratitude, I couldn't help but be charmed by him all over again. There was just something about this interesting Fae that took my breath away. And even if he didn't have a scent that a soul mate would have, I couldn't deny the music he called our heartsong.

7

TOBIAS

*C*aleb and Helena had been saying goodbye for over
an hour, but I hesitated to rush them. I felt badly,
knowing that I was the instrument that would separate them
forever, but at the same time, I was overjoyed to know that
Caleb's life would be saved now that he would be coming
home with me.

My wings fluttered on either side of the openings in the
shirt I had been told was called a tank top. Caleb had
purchased it for me to wear on our trip back to the portal.
Even if nobody could see us, he said he did not like the idea
of me traveling across the globe with no shirt on. Humans
could be so provincial at times, but I found his possessive
side to be completely adorable. As I watched them embrace, I
tried not to worry about the passing time. I had allotted
enough time for our leavetaking, since I had assumed it
would go exactly like this.

The two of them rocked from side to side as they hugged.
Helena turned to glance at me, then froze in place—her eyes
nearly bulging out of her head as she stared at me. Caleb
took a step back, his face filled with confusion as he looked

back and forth between the two of us. "Why are you acting weird, Hells? You're looking at Tobias like he's suddenly sprouted a second head or something."

Helena shook her head. "Nope, it's not a head he's sprouted. Even though you told me, and I knew you couldn't possibly be making it up..." She paused and took a breath, shaking her head as she stared at me in amazement. "To actually see the evidence with my own eyes is nothing short of amazing."

I followed her line of sight to where she stared at my wings fluttering behind me. "Oh! You can see my wings! That is rare for a human unless you have bonded to me, which we obviously have not."

Helena blushed as she shot me a shy smile. "I may or may not have lit a candle last night and sent a prayer out into the universe for proof that Caleb would be okay. I think maybe seeing this is my wish being granted." She took a step toward me, lifting a hand without seeming to realize it. "Would it be all right if I maybe just... I mean... they're just so pretty and..."

I threw back my head with a laugh. "Go on then, give my wings a touch. After you have looked and touched your fill, I am afraid we will need to say our final goodbye because time grows short and we have to be at the portal before the moon reaches its apex."

Caleb threw his arm around Helena's waist. "Come on, girlie. Just reach out and grab the edge of a wing. Take a handful and stroke it. Wait until you see how soft they are, it will blow your ever-loving mind."

Turning around, I arched my back a little so my wings were within reach. Helena's touch was tentative at first, then more confident as she stroked and ran a reverent hand over the edges of my wings. After she had satisfied her curiosity, I turned around and gave her a hug of my own as

I chuckled against her ear. "Go ahead, ask all your questions."

She stood back, rubbing her hands together almost glee-fully. "I don't have time for you to answer even a third of my questions, so let me just ask the important ones. Is it possible to break a wing? How do you sleep with them? I would think you'd roll over on them and get all caught up or something. Oh, and were you born with wings? How does that work, coming out of the birth canal?"

I threw my head back and laughed, then turned around again and retracted my wings. I heard a sharp intake of breath from each of them. Caleb was familiar with my wings disappearing, but he had never seen them when I tucked them away, letting them sink into my flesh and disappear as if being neatly folded into a compartment.

Helena walked right up and pressed a hand on my back, running her fingertips over each of the lacy birthmarks that appeared when my wings were not extended. "If I hadn't seen it with my own eyes, I'd think you were pulling one over on me. This is fantastic."

"All right, all right. Quit handling the merchandise," Caleb said with a laugh as he batted her hands away.

I turned back around to see them pretending to fight as they batted and swatted at each other's hands. After a moment, they were hugging again. When they pulled apart, Helena turned back to me with an expectant smile. "So, does that mean you don't have to worry about wings getting crushed in the birth canal?"

"Not to my knowledge, no." I shrugged a shoulder and tried to quickly answer her questions. "My wings are an extension of myself, but I can tuck them away at will. When Fae younglings are born, we look like any other child, I expect. Our parent calls forth our majick and forces our wings to appear the first time. After that, the birthmark

71

forms once they retract again. And before you ask, most Fae babies do not use their wings again until they start walking."

Helena nodded solemnly. "That probably helps keep them from smothering themselves in their sleep, I would think. You never said if your wings can be broken. Is that a concern with little Fae?"

I shook my head. "No, our wings are soft, as you felt for yourself. When they get smashed, they simply crumple like velvet. But usually, we will retract them before that can happen. As you can probably imagine, we Fae are rightly proud of our wings. The color patterns are unique, like your human fingerprints. The colors themselves generally run within family lines, but the actual patterning of the hues and tones are what make us unique. My wing colors come from my parents—the teals are from my mother, and the purples are from my father."

"Thank you so much for sharing that with me." Helena stooped to pick up Caleb's small bag of items he had decided to bring along. There was not much, since he would not need his human clothes in my realm. As I had told him, the synthetic fabrics would not be comfortable there anyway. He had surprised me when he had packed the turquoise bandanna that he had protested every time Helena had tied it around his neck, but I imagined it was probably a sentimental choice. The only other items he had packed were pictures of the two of them, and older photographs of his parents, along with a few other personal possessions.

As he took custody of the bag, Caleb gave his friend one final hug and pressed a kiss to her cheek. "I'm sure gonna miss you, Hells. I love you so much. Thank you for being my family."

Helena's eyes were bright with unshed tears as she wagged her finger in Caleb's face. "Oh, no. You don't get to thank me for being your family, doofus. Family just is, you know? Just as we are and evermore shall be. You don't need to miss me, because you'll be carrying a bit of me in your heart just like I will have a piece of you in mine. Besides, we have those cool little magic baubles that Tobias made us, remember? Anytime you get homesick for my ugly mug, just hold it up to the light and let it do its thing."

Caleb reached up and wiped a stray tear from her cheek with the pad of his thumb. "Always the tough girl. It's okay to admit that you'll miss me too. But you're right, we were always meant to be family and we always will remain so—whether we are together or separated. Blessed be, Hells."

"Blessed be, Caley," Helena echoed. She smiled softly and leaned forward to kiss Caleb's cheek. "And yes, I will miss you. I love you too, and don't you dare ever think otherwise. But Caley, I'm good with this separation, I really am. I'd prepared myself to see you die, and instead I'll get to know that you're going to have a full, magical life with your sexy Fae-mate for a playmate." She waggled her eyebrows, giggling at Caleb's groan. "What, you don't like my rhyme? Don't be jelly. You wish you had my flow."

"I'm pretty sure you don't have the first clue of what *flow* is, Hells. We discussed this when you tried to do open mic night a few years ago, remember?" As if he were aware of the time, Caleb took a deep breath and walked over to my side. "We could stand here and tease all day to prolong my departure, but it won't make it any easier. So let's just say that we'll remember each other fondly—and always with a smile—so that we can be on our way."

Helena turned to me. "Take care of him, Tobias. I know from what I've read in the leaves that you don't need that particular admonishment, but I need to give it anyway. It's my duty as his best friend and unofficial sister. Just love him for me and make sure you give him a hard time every once in a while. He needs to be teased, otherwise he'll get cocky and full of himself—kinda like you, now that I think about it." She turned and flashed a wink at Caleb. "Come to think of it, that little cocky streak of yours will make you a perfect citizen of the Fae realm, if Tobias here is anything to go on."

Caleb snorted, shaking his head as he rolled his eyes. "Cocky? Yeah, sure. Because I'm the one that's always been full of myself." Helena laughed as the two of them shared a smile that only friends of long duration can possess.

I struck my best preening pose and glared down at her haughtily. "Are you calling me cocky, little girl?"

"Yeah, I'm pretty sure that's what I said." She laughed as she took a step back. "Okay, get out of here while we're laughing. There's nothing worse than a teary goodbye."

I scooped Caleb up in my arms, cradling him against my chest while he in turn held onto his bag with a death grip with one hand, while wrapping his other around my neck. I gave my wings a flutter and lifted from the ground, shooting Helena my cockiest grin when she squealed and clapped her hands with sheer joy.

Shielding her eyes from the sun, she gazed up at us. "Aren't you worried about being seen, Tobias? Even if humans can't see your wings, surely someone will notice two men flying overhead."

"Aye, but that is where my cloaking spell comes in. Now you see me," I cloaked us and watched her eyes widen as we disappeared from view. "And now you don't."

She laughed, even as she shook her head. "I don't know if it's disconcerting or just weird as hell to hear your voice and not see you. Caleb, say goodbye so I can hear your voice floating around without being able to see you. In fact, don't drop your invisibility shield, or cloak, or whatever you call it, Tobias. This way, I'll be able to pretend that you're always right out here, still invisible and just outside of view."

"Goodbye, Hells. I love you. Whenever you hear a whisper on the wind, just pretend it's me hovering nearby shrouded in an invisibility cloak. I like that idea." Caleb spoke cheerfully, despite the tears that were now streaking down his face. He looked to me with a nod as if to say, 'let's go.' As I rose a little higher, he called back to Helena one final time. "Blessed be, Hells."

She lifted a hand in farewell, the smile on her face in direct contradiction to the tears streaming down her face as she echoed his sentiment. "Blessed be, Caley. Blessed be."

When we arrived at the portal, Caleb seemed almost grateful when I set him down. He grinned as he took my hand. "I'm pretty sure that entire trip took less than three minutes at best, but at the same time my brain feels like I just took a long journey and I'm relieved to have my feet on the ground again. Is that weird?"

"If you ask me, it's probably mental more than anything. I have to admit though, I've often felt the same way after a dreamscape that takes place in a faraway land." We both turned to see Sammy speaking as he and his brothers approached, along with the rest of their group.

They all started to form a circle around us where we stood a meter or so from the portal. Easton had a more formal air about him than he had previously when I had seen him. He stepped forward while the shifters took each other's hands and closed the wide circle that encapsulated the three of us and the portal.

Easton looked back and forth between me and Caleb for a moment before speaking. "Does the fact that the two of you are standing here suggest that you have both decided to accept our offer? And if so, does this mean that you are

75

willing to trade your soul for the boon of immortality, Caleb?"

Caleb started to accept, when one of the shifters—a small omega who we had not met yet—released the hands he was holding and stepped forward, sniffing the air. "I'm sorry, but I feel like I should interrupt real quick. My name is Aaron, and I am a healer. Before you accept, I need to ask if you know that you're pregnant, and are effectively deciding for both of you? If you make this choice, you're also sealing the fate of your pup to not have a human soul but rather to live as an immortal Fae. I can't heal you since that's not your fate, but I could probably extend your life long enough to give birth, if Tobias would rather stay here. I don't want to ruin your plans, but I feel like I need to make the offer."

My heart raced as I heard those words, while my stomach flipped and did funny things. Should we stay? Was it fair to rob our child of the human experience? But on the other hand, if we stayed then we would be certainly robbing him of one of his parents. And did I really want to stay here? Cursed to be ever alone after my mate would eventually die, leaving me a world away from my own family who would dearly love to know my child? I was vaguely aware of my nerves disrupting the heartsong. The strained notes were making the melody discordant until Caleb squeezed my hand with a soft smile, instantly calming me before he turned to answer Aaron.

"No, but thank you for telling me about the pup. Staying here would be selfish, and being pregnant gives me all the more reason to cross realms. My child is half Fae anyway, so why wouldn't I want them to live in their homeland? Also, why would I curse my child and my beloved to live without me when I can do such a simple thing to be with them? Please, let me cross over and begin my family with Tobias. This is my wish."

Aaron's face lit up with a broad smile. "Awesome, I figured that would probably be your decision, but I still wouldn't have felt right to have not at least offered the information." He gave a cute little wave before going back to rejoin his circle.

Easton turned to Caleb. "Before you leave us, I have one more boon to offer. Would you care to have a Fae form of your own, or would you rather retain your spirit animal?"

Caleb's eyes widened as he shook his head. "No, thank you. I need my wolf! He is a part of me, just as I am a part of him." He bit his lip and cocked his head to the side for a moment as he studied Easton before speaking again. "Do you have to do anything special to remove my soul, and if so... will it hurt? I don't care if it does, I just want to prepare myself."

A bright, sparkling laugh rippled through the air as Easton chuckled. "No, you won't even notice it. We've spelled the portal so that it will happen instantaneously as you cross. You won't feel any differently or even notice the loss— although you'll probably feel a bit more pep in your step, because you won't be aging in human terms anymore."

The one called Sammy spoke again. "As much as I hate to spoil the fun of you figuring it all out for yourself, can I give you a tip? When you shift for the first time in the Fae realm, make sure you speak to your mate. You might be surprised by the sounds that come out of your mouth. Also, when you shift there, you won't need to dress and undress. You'll be able to simply think your clothes onto your body as you shift, or off as the case may be. These are the only hints I'm allowed to give you. You're going to have so much fun. Enjoy your new life with your mate, Tobias and Caleb."

With that, Caleb and I shared a quick decisive nod and walked toward the portal hand-in-hand. I took one last glance back, only to see the smiling faces of these gracious souls who had so kindly and wonderfully changed both our lives. I felt him squeezing my hand and glanced back down at my mate. He leaned up on tiptoe for a kiss, his eyes sparkling with the excitement of the moment.

I bent and brushed a kiss over his lips. As soon as we broke apart, Caleb glanced back over his shoulder and waved to the circle. "Before we go, I just want to say thank you." They all beamed back at us and nodded toward the portal while murmuring their goodbyes.

The moon was directly overhead and I knew the time was growing short. We needed to go, so I gave Caleb's hand a squeeze and stepped toward the entrance to the portal. "Are you ready to change your life, mate?"

"You bet I am. Let's do this, angel boy." I was still smiling at his words as we took our first step together toward our new future.

8

CALEB

*a*s I crossed over the portal, the difference was like night and day. I felt like Dorothy as I looked around at the colorful scenery—I definitely wasn't in Kansas anymore, metaphorically speaking. Tobias stood there quietly while I looked around the area. The portal was gone when I glanced back over my shoulder. All I could see behind us now was a field of brightly colored flowers.

Even the sky itself was different from everything I knew. The blues were deeper, yet as it faded toward the edge of the horizon, it felt like I was looking at a sunset. *No, that wasn't quite right.* It was more like the way the sky looked in pictures I'd seen of forest fires. So many different corals and pinks and lavenders blending beautifully together before moving up into a vibrant blue.

I blinked and turned away from the bright sun, only to see it reappear on the opposite side of the horizon. How was that possible? When I looked back, the sun was where it had been. I nearly gave myself a neck ache as I jerked my head back and forth several times before finally realizing that there were two suns. I heard laughter and turned to see Tobias doubled over.

When he saw my playful glare, he held up a hand. "My apologies. I had not thought about how my world would look through your eyes, or I would have tried to prepare you. We have the twin suns to light our days. When night inevitably comes, you will see our five moons. Technically you only see three of them because two of them are playful bastards and only appear on the clearest of nights."

I took a deep breath of the fresh, clean air and felt almost giddy. I made a mental note to ask if the oxygen was the same, because my giddiness could easily be explained by the fact that I was seeing a completely new world. But oxygen-rich air could also explain it. I was pretty sure I was safe here though, or the legacy pack wouldn't have let me cross the portal. At least... I was pretty sure they wouldn't. At any rate, this was still better than dying, even if I did need to learn to process oxygen differently. Was that even a thing? Gah. So many questions.

I held a hand toward the sky, needing to get an answer to that before we moved any further. "Why isn't the sky blue? At first I thought it was a sunset, but the sun—or suns, I guess I should say—are too high in the sky right now."

Tobias shrugged. "I suppose a more scientific mind would tell you there is more dust in our atmosphere, but I would not underestimate the amount of majicks in the air either. Come, let us walk some more so you can explore further. I would offer to fly us to my home—since we are a fair distance from town—but I believe you would probably rather be free to take everything in."

I remembered him telling me the story of when the portal had appeared in his bedroom and glanced back over my shoulder toward the field of flowers where the portal had dropped us off. "Are there different portal exits and entrances? I thought you said the portal was in your bedroom?"

"In that instance it was, but not always. The doorway to your world has been sealed for so long that I had not ever expected to see it again. But the way it worked when it was operational in the past was simply that it would appear and disappear at will, going wherever it was meant to be." Tobias struggled to explain, finally ending his thought with a shrug.

I nodded with understanding. "It's okay to just say it's a magical thing, if you want. I'm pretty sure that probably describes most of your world anyway."

Tobias laughed and nodded his agreement. "Aye, that will likely be a good answer for a fair number of your questions." As we walked along a hard-packed dirt path, I couldn't tear my eyes away from all the wonders we passed. The trees were similar to the ones I was used to—in shape anyway. The trunks grew in a variety of colors, and the leaves were either a paler shade than the trunk, or a contrasting color. I saw purple trunks with orange leaves, and blue trunks with pale baby blue leaves. It was just a riotous rainbow of color and I couldn't wait to see more.

We passed a pond with such crystal blue waters that I could see the fish swimming. I started to ask about whether the fish were edible here, or merely to be admired—when a bright red fish jumped out of the water in a high arc. I was admiring its beauty when a loud screeching was heard overhead as a large pink bird swooped out of nowhere and swallowed the fish whole before flying off again. Tobias took one look at my face and started laughing.

"What's so funny?" I asked with a snort of laughter.

"The look on your face was priceless," Tobias explained between bouts of mirth. "Yes, the circle of life works here too —as you just witnessed."

"No fair. You're totally reading my mind, aren't you?

What did you call it? Gleaning information or something like that?"

Tobias grinned and flashed me a wink. "Yes, that is what I call it, but no—I would not do that to you without your permission. It is considered rude here to read the minds of friends and family if you have not asked first."

After we passed a pond, I saw another field of the rainbow-colored flowers that had been behind us when we arrived. "Ooh, I want to get a look at those. They're just so pretty. What are those, some sort of a tulip or something? They look just like tulips, but it's crazy to see them growing wild in so many different colors."

"Wait, those are not at all what you think they—" Tobias tried to stop me but I was already running toward the field. I stopped at the edge and squatted to get a closer look. Each flower had twin stamens that were kicking and waving in the breeze. I went to stroke one with the back of my finger and jerked my hand back when it kicked me!

Before I could turn to say something to Tobias, one of those big pink birds swooped down and plucked a pretty pink flower in its beak. It tossed it up in the air as if it were going to eat it. Luckily, the flower missed its beak and fell.

Stretching out a hand, I easily caught the flower before it hit the ground. I waved at the bird to shoo it away. "Shame on you! You're not supposed to eat pretty things like this. Go over to the pond and look for a stinky fish." I heard Tobias laughing as I scolded the bird and nearly missed the flower turn itself over in my palm.

I stared in wonder as a tiny little lady stood there staring up at me; it was like holding a six-inch action figure come to life. I couldn't hear what she was saying, so I brought my hand closer to hear her—and get a better look. What I had thought was a tulip was actually her skirt. She brushed it down demurely as she chattered, but I couldn't understand a word she was saying. It sounded like the chittering of a squirrel, rather than any language I'd ever heard. Her dress was a pale pink, while her skin tone was almost a pastel green. Now that I saw her more closely, it was easy to understand why I'd mistaken her for a flower.

Oh, dear. No wonder she'd kicked me! I'd been brushing my finger over her leg like a giant perv. When I heard a sigh, I looked over to see Tobias squatting beside me. He waved a hand toward the tulip girl with a resigned look in his eye. "Remember how I told you that I am Fae and not a fairy? This is a fairy. Now do you see the difference?" He flashed me a wink to let me know he was teasing about our past conversation.

"She's fantastic. Are all fairies girls? And why was she planted in the ground? That's weird." I knew I was rambling, but I couldn't help it.

Before he could answer, the entire field of flowers dipped to the side as if hit by a gust of wind. The flowers all flipped over then floated up in the air and flew directly at me. I stood to my feet, cradling the small fairy against my chest as if to protect her from the onslaught of her people as they rushed toward us like a mighty wind.

Tobias chuckled as he also stood, taking a step back away from me, like a six-foot rat escaping this sinking ship. "Just stay in one spot and don't move. They want to check you out and reward you for saving one of their own."

Despite the nearly microscopic size of their wings, it truly felt like I was standing in a gale force wind as they came right at me and flew around me in a tunnel of air. It was like I was standing in the eye of a tornado—except instead of hearing a howling wind, it sounded more like a million tiny bells ringing, and that almost zipping whoosh of a sound that I'd always associated with a hummingbird.

The fairy I was holding floated up in front of my face and

threw handfuls of pollen—or maybe it was pixie dust—at me. I sneezed when it went right up my nose, sending the little fairy backwards into the twirling wall of her cohorts that were fluttering around me and blocking out the sunlight.

The fairy bounced off the spinning wall of fairies and appeared right back in my face. She was laughing and this time flew directly over my head before a deluge of pixie dust —or whatever it was called—showered down over me. The wall pressed closer, so close that I could feel the flutters of their wings. It was as if a million butterflies were dancing over my skin. It tickled in a way, and somehow managed to feel even a bit indecent... especially when I felt them brushing over my bottom.

It felt like it went on indefinitely until all at once, they broke away and the wall dissipated as if it had never been. The little fairy I'd saved was the only one remaining as the rest took off and disappeared into the horizon. Fluttering next to my face like a hummingbird, she seemed to be moving with me every time I turned my head. I looked at Tobias in confusion—and more than a little bit of desperation—and mouthed the word *help*.

Tobias roared with laughter then motioned toward my body. "You have been given a gift, mate. I am surprised you have not felt the difference. Look down and see what they have given you."

My eyebrows were pinched together as I frowned in confusion, but I looked down as he'd suggested. It took a few seconds for my brain to make sense of what I was seeing. Gone were my old jeans and T-shirt that I'd worn for travel; in their place was a pristine, white linen pants suit.

The pants were loose fitting and flared at the ankles, while the shirt was a sleeveless tunic that ended about an inch above the waist of the pants so that a flash of skin showed. It was a genderless outfit, but yet I felt like I'd borrowed something from Helena's closet. I'd never worn something so loose fitting before, but I had to admit that it felt pretty comfortable.

As soon as I thought about the comfort level, it occurred to me that I was feeling a lot freer in the crotch region. I did my best to ignore the fairy fluttering beside my face as I discreetly adjusted my junk. Tobias was obviously waiting for my reaction because when my jaw fell open, he started laughing so hard that he fell on his ass.

Yep. He fell right there in the middle of the road—which totally served him right. I stood there, leaning my weight onto one hip as I crossed my arms over my chest and watched him lose his shit.

Once he calmed down, I simply lifted a brow. "Are you quite finished, or did you want to laugh some more?"

Tobias sat up, wiping his eyes with the back of his hand as he shook his head. "No, if I laugh anymore I will most likely piss myself. I am sorry, mate, the look on your face..." His voice trailed off as he shook his head again. "I am sorry. I cannot discuss it or I will start laughing again."

I couldn't even pretend to be angry for another second as I started snickering when I looked down at my pants, my reaction coming out in a rush of words. "I can't believe I just totally had my clothes ripped off then got felt up by a million fairies. At least they dressed me in pretty clothes as their thank you, because—that's not creepy. Please tell me that's not something I can look forward to every day. Also, can you see my balls? This linen is kind of sheer and I'm pretty sure based on your laughter that you are aware that I'm now going commando. *Freaking fairies.* And what in the heck happened to my own clothes?"

Tobias stared a little too long at my crotch before shaking his head. "No, I think you are sufficiently decent and will not be giving anybody a free show. And no, you do not need to worry about that happening every day. A new suit of clothing is considered a fine gift. This was their thank you for saving their sister. They probably went a little overboard because you are new to our world. As for your clothing, consider it gone. They likely used its fibers and fairy dust to make this new replacement."

I stared at him for a minute, trying to process that statement. "Do I look weird or something? How would they know I'm new to this world?"

Tobias smiled patiently. "Sweetheart, none of us have seen a human in more than a millennia and suddenly here you are… and as for young fairies like those, they have never seen one of your kind before. Of course you are new, how could you be anything else? The entire region will be abuzz before we reach my abode with the news of your arrival. You will be the most exciting thing to have happened around here since our last multi-lunar eclipse."

The little pink fairy was still fluttering beside my head as I walked closer to Tobias and stretched a hand out to help him up. I darted my eyes in her direction as he accepted my hand and stood. "How long is my biggest fan going to be stalking me? And also, why did you say that she was their sister? Is that how they refer to each other? As sisters and brothers?"

Tobias offered his arm. I took it and fell into step with him as we continued our walk. He smiled as he explained, "She is literally their sister. Fairies reproduce once every thousand years or so, sometimes more often if their population dwindles thanks to natural predators like the Fufu bird you saw. Rather than carrying them like most mammals, fairies lay eggs like a spider. They can have nests with several thousand children hatching at once. The siblings spend most of their lives together, almost like a flock. Which is how we refer to them, by the way—a flock of fairies."

"What the flock?" I grinned, unable to resist the pun. "Okay. Now you've got to be pulling my leg. Fairies come from a nest of eggs like a spider? And then all the thousands of siblings stick together? How do they ever meet other fairies to reproduce?"

I froze mid-step and tugged his arm as a horrible thought occurred to me. I lowered my voice just in case the fairy understood English. "They don't... you know..." I paused and glanced back at the fairy before finishing my thought. "What I mean is, it's not incestuous, right? Although, would it be considered inbreeding if it's only a matter of laying eggs and then I would assume... er, inseminating them?" Tobias started laughing, but I tugged on his arm to make him stop so I could voice my next thought. "How do they even inseminate the eggs? I have so many questions now. Do the female fairies lay a bunch of eggs and then a male comes along and just like, I don't know—jacks off and sprays his load over the eggs? Or does gender matter? Are there male omega fairies who lay eggs?"

Tobias stared at me for a long moment and shook his head. "Yes, I am pretty sure it does not work like that here— or in any other world, for that matter. No, there are no omegas. Only females with eggs. And no, they do it the old-fashioned way and then she lays her eggs that have already been inseminated." He shuddered and took a resolute step forward.

My hand was still wrapped around his arm, so he was tugging me along with him; whether or not he was aware of this fact, I couldn't say for sure since he was stuck on the whole fairy sex thing. Tobias groaned as he shook his head. "The mental imagery this conversation has provided me is unfair. Remind me... why are we talking about the reproduction habits of fairies?"

I shrugged, then cast a guilty glance toward my little fairy stalker before looking back at Tobias with a wince. "I really shouldn't be discussing this in front of her, should I? Can she even understand me?" A tiny chittering sound answered that question for me. I glanced out of the corner of my eye just in time to see her turning somersaults in the air as she giggled.

After he got done laughing some more, Tobias released my arm and put his hand around my shoulder. "Please do not feel badly, mate. It is to be expected that you would be confused. This is an entirely new world for you. As for your stalker? I would suggest you pick out a name for her. They do not generally take names when part of the flock. It is not until they separate and begin to lead their own life and look for a mate that they take a name for themselves. And as for her hanging around—you saved her life, so now she is yours. She will stay by your side and look out for you, protect you, and help you in any way she can."

I was horrified by that idea. "But I didn't do anything special! She's not a house elf, she doesn't need to serve me for life. If she were a little bigger I'd offer to give her a sock if that would be enough to free her, but I don't think they make socks that small."

Tobias didn't get the reference, so he must not have tapped into any brains that were thinking of *Harry Potter* when he had been gleaning cultural information. I made a mental note to explain it later and pushed on. "And why would I name her? That's not my right. Heck, I didn't even know she was a living being. I thought she was a flower. Which reminds me, why the heck were they posing as flowers anyway?"

"There were a lot of thoughts there, mate. I am not sure if I followed all of them, but I can explain the flowers. It is pretty simple actually. They clean themselves by flying over the pond and taking a quick dip into the water. As they fly away they are mostly dried by the sun but their private regions do not quite get aired out. They stand on their heads in the field to... erm, finish freshening up a bit."

I turned to look at my new personal fairy, who was nodding in agreement with everything Tobias had just said. There was no way I was going to comment on the public airing of fairy junk, so I just blew out a breath and looked at her.

"I feel like Tinkerbell would be too obvious a name, so what do you think if I call you Pinky? I feel like that's your favorite color, and there is a famous lady back in my world named Pink—so it definitely works as a name. What do you think?" I felt like a crazy person to be having a one-way conversation with this chittering little exhibitionist fairy, but she clapped her hands and spun in a circle—obviously approving of the name I'd bequeathed her. I gave a decisive nod. "Alrighty then, Pinky it is."

Tobias huffed as we got closer to the outskirts of a quaint looking little town. "I can't believe I'm bringing a fairy home to live with me. When my family finds out, they are going to have a field day."

I tripped over my foot and nearly fell face first at the mention of his family. Tobias easily caught me and helped me find my balance while Pinky made alarming noises and flew up and down as if inspecting my body before settling back beside my face with a chittering noise that sounded like relief. "Are you okay, mate? What happened there? Did you nearly fall because of a rock?"

Since I wasn't about to tell him that I'd nearly tripped because the mention of his family had scared the crap out of me, I just nodded and went along with the whole rock thing. The truth of the matter? I hadn't stopped to think too much about his family yet. What if they didn't like me? Or even worse—what if they hated me?

I tried to keep my tone casual as I turned to Tobias, not

wanting him to suspect my concerns. "Will your family be there when we arrive? You don't live with them, do you? Not that I would mind, I'm just curious." I was thinking about the big nest of fairies who lived in a flock, so I figured it was a reasonable question to ask if he lived with his family.

"Good gracious, no. My family lives nearby, but I have not lived with them in centuries. The reason we are so close is thanks to the fact that we live apart. Have no fear, you will certainly see your fill of them. Especially once they return home and learn of your existence. My mother will have a fit that she was not here to greet and welcome you."

My stomach settled once I learned that his family wouldn't be there to greet me. I was doing my best to keep my heart rate steady so the damn heartsong wouldn't give me away, but I was frankly a little surprised he hadn't noticed the uptick in the rhythm.

Although, now that I thought about it, my heart had probably been racing with varying degrees of excitement or terror pretty much since I'd stepped through the portal, so maybe he wasn't noticing it right now. I took a calming breath before speaking. "Where are they right now, if they won't be here for me to meet today?"

While he explained about his family being expert potion and tool makers—or *smiths*, thus his surname—and described a hunt for an elusive crystal his mother needed, I was ashamed to say that I only listened with half an ear. I tried to absorb the information while also trying not to stare at the adorable town we were entering.

The dirt road we'd been traveling gave way to cobblestone. All the buildings, whether residential or business, reminded me of Smurf Village from the old cartoon. They were all round, white buildings with brightly colored mushroom-top roofs.

I really wanted to ask if Fae children ever climbed to the

top and slid down. And if so, did the dip at the edge keep them from falling over or propel them into a wider arc as they went flying? Instead of voicing my thoughts, I remembered I was a grown up and asked a completely different—and mature—question. "When do you expect them to return?"

He thought about that for a second then shook his head. "I am not sure how long I was gone since time is fluid here. But they were following a lead that led them to the outskirts of the umber region of the high North, so who is to say?"

"And your entire family went on this hunt?" I wanted to ask why he called it a hunt, but was afraid to know the answer, given that I'd already witnessed flowers that turned out to be upside-down exhibitionist fairies instead of tulips with twin stamens.

Tobias was unaware of my train of thought. "Oh, yes. The entire family goes on the hunt when rare ingredients are spotted. The only reason I did not go was because I have been contemplating a different career path."

I turned to look at him curiously. "A different career path? After a lifetime of working with your family? That's interesting. Did something happen to push you in that direction, or is there something different you've always wanted to do?"

Tobias lifted a shoulder into a shrug. "Not really. In fact, if I left the clan guild, I do not know what I would do. I have been at loose ends for the past few decades. I had felt like my life was about to change, and I guess I just assumed it was my career."

He flashed me a wink. "I never would have guessed that my heartsong was on the horizon, or that I would be looking forward to fatherhood. I cannot wait for my family to come home; they are going to be so happy for us. Just watch out for my mom, she is going to be obnoxious when she hears that she is to have a grand youngling."

Watch out for his mom? She was going to be obnoxious? I shot him a nervous smile and tried to keep my heart rate from betraying my anxiety. Pinky must have picked up on my subtle cues, because she splashed another dollop of pixie dust in my face. When I sneezed from the bit that blew up my nose, she just made a chittering noise as if she were blessing me. If they even sneezed here... who knows, maybe she thought it was cute.

Tobias wasn't quite as unaware as I'd thought. He tightened his arm that was resting around my shoulders, squeezing me against his side as he brushed a kiss over my temple. "Do not worry, I am only teasing. My mother is going to adore you, mate. How could she not? You are my mate."

9

TOBIAS

"No, Pinky. You know you are not allowed in our private chambers." I glared at the irritating fairy who was hovering in our doorway. I ignored her chittering and firmly shook my head. "Caleb is not only yours to protect, he is also my mate. I am willing to share him with you, but not within our bedchamber." I rolled my eyes when she chittered some more and reluctantly nodded when she refused to leave. "Fine, I will ask him."

I turned to where Caleb was sitting on our bed, watching us with an amused smile. "Your blasted fairy companion wishes to know how she can be of service while you slumber."

Caleb turned to Pinky with a look of dismay. "No, pretty girl. You need to rest. Don't you like the little fairy cottage we made you?"

Pinky's glowering visage turned into a bright smile for her beloved Caleb. She did a somersault, clapping her hands and sending bits of fairy dust flying through the air. I had to admit, the damn fairy was more than a little bit adorable—especially when she was fawning over my mate. She might constantly be underfoot, but I could not fault her taste. When I was not paying close enough attention, she buzzed right into my face and rapped me on the nose as she chittered.

"Fine, I will let him know." I groaned, then glanced back to a grinning Caleb. "Pinky wants you to know that she adores her little cottage. However, she does not require the same amount of slumber as her precious human. Caleb, my love. I beg of you, please give her a task to perform so that she will take her leave."

Caleb watched me for a moment, his eyes twinkling with amusement. At first, I thought he was going to tease me, but he seemed to think better of it as he waved a hand toward Pinky. "All right, pretty girl. Why don't you go work in the nursery tonight? The crib that Tobias built is nice and solid, but I would prefer a more delicate look. Perhaps you might find a way to paint it white? Maybe put a few flowers or other bits of decoration along the head and footboards? I don't know why, but I really feel like we're going to have a girl. I want her to feel like a princess."

Pinky was all over that. She did a few more aerial somersaults, clapping her hands and chittering so fast that even I could barely interpret what she was saying. Though I had no problem comprehending the patronizing smile she shot my way before flying off into the next room where we were setting up our youngling's nursery. I closed the door firmly behind her and turned the lock before breathing a sigh of relief.

"She's not that bad. I wish you two would quit your silly rivalry. Come on, angel boy. Come snuggle with me." Caleb shimmied out of his clothes, pushing them off the side of the bed before he slid under the covers. I was already undressing as I crossed the room.

"I never said that she is bad, just that she never seems to

give us a moment's peace." My tone was sulky as I climbed into bed with a matching pout on my face.

Before I had completely stretched out, Caleb was climbing on top of me. Bracing himself on his forearms, he bent to kiss my face as he rolled his hips to press his erect length against mine. "I don't see her in here now, so why don't we forget about anyone and anything but us for a few minutes?"

I quirked a brow. "A few minutes? Surely you are under-estimating me, mate. A few minutes is barely enough time for me to get properly hard, it would take an entire night to sate my desire for you—and even then it would take but a brief respite before I would need to start again."

Caleb stared at me for a moment then started laughing. "Say that again, I love that cocky arrogance. Not to mention how casually you throw off the cheesiest lines. Or, you could do less talking and more kissing? That always works."

I cradled his face in my hands and closed the short distance between his lips and mine. When his tongue thrust into my mouth, a spark shot straight to my balls—a sure sign that he was right. More kissing definitely worked. Caleb moaned into my mouth as I slipped a hand between us to grip both of our cocks in my fist. The pre-cum was flowing from our tips, aiding me as I stroked back-and-forth along our lengths.

"Yesss, angel boy. Just like that." Caleb broke our kiss to speak, moving his mouth along my jaw and down my neck, peppering kisses as he went. His hands were everywhere; my hair, my shoulders, along my sides and back up my chest to tweak my nipples with those nimble fingertips. And through it all, our heartsong rang true.

Before I could take things into a more intimate direction, my balls pulled tight and I could feel my orgasm fast approaching. I tried to pull back and slow down to stretch out the moment. I nearly succeeded, until my imp of a mate decided to nip at the point of my ear. Even then, I was almost able to stay strong, until he began flicking his tongue across the point.

Fireballs barreled down my spine and straight to my cock. I barely had time to gasp out his name before I was shooting my full load across our chests and stomachs. Caleb grunted and rocked his hips faster as I tightened my fist and flicked my thumb over his tip. It was not long before he was stiffening and calling my name while splashing cum over my skin. After he finished, Caleb relaxed and stretched over me like a limp noodle.

We lay there for a few heartbeats before Caleb started chuckling. "What was that you were saying about a few minutes and underestimating you? And for the record, which one of us came first? Remind me… I'm not sure I'm remembering correctly."

I roared with laughter as I rolled us over until he was on his back and I was caging him in with my body as I leaned on my elbows and peered down at him. "Aye, fair enough. But we should consider that bit of trickery you pulled."

Caleb grinned unrepentantly. "Hey, it's not my fault that the delectable tips of your ears are an erogenous zone. Who would've thought there were so many nerve endings in those little points?" I bent to kiss him, unable to resist the siren call of his soft lips. When I pulled away, his eyes lit with curiosity as though something had occurred to him—an expression I was familiar with after sharing fifteen slumbers with my inquisitive mate. He was enjoying every moment as he soaked up the wonders of this new world.

"It just dawned on me that you referred to a unit of time earlier when you said few minutes." He shook his head. "Not important. My point is that I've started to realize that time stands still or something like that, in this world. You guys don't even have clocks here. How does that work? More than once, I've heard you guys note time passing by how many slumbers you've had—which is a very weird way of keeping track of time passing, if you ask me."

I soaked in his words and tried to think of a proper response. "Fair point. When I said a *few minutes*, I was using a time reference from your world, not mine. Time is relative here. Things happen when they are meant to, and we just go along with it. It is day for as long as the suns wish to shine, and then it is night for however long the moons wish to take control. We sleep and wake when our bodies demand it and whether there are suns or moons. It is just the way of things."

Caleb rolled off me and settled onto his side. He absently stroked the trail of hair leading downward from my navel as he thought about what I had said. He looked up with a sudden grin, and I thought we were still having the conversation about time when he spoke. "I can't believe I never noticed this before... it's just so sparkly. I swear, everything gets curiouser and curiouser."

Sparkly? I started to ask what in the world he meant, when I noticed he was picking dried cum from the trail of hair. I snickered, stretching an arm over my head as I flashed him a grin. "Aye, my cum rivals that of a unicorn, is that what you were thinking?"

His head popped up, a look of wonder crossing his face as his jaw fell open. "Unicorns exist? You absolutely need to show me one."

My snickers turned into a full rolling laugh. "No, I was just teasing. We have many wonders in this realm, but unicorns are not one of them—more's the pity. As for my sparkling jizz, how else is one to make a magical youngling without a bit of glitter?"

We were still laughing when the room suddenly went

dark. Caleb clutched for my hand, cuddling up against me suddenly. "Where did the light go?"

I bent to kiss his forehead. "Come with me, let me show you to the window—I believe that night has fallen at last."

Caleb allowed me to lead him from the bed to peer out the window. He gazed in awe at the nighttime sky. Unlike in his world where it went an inky black, ours was a range of darkest reds to royal purples and deep shades of blue.

"It's almost like a sunset, but darker. How is there still so much color in the sky?" His voice was filled with wonder as he looked back-and-forth between the three visible moons. He shuddered at the sight of the nearest moon that was so close that it took up a large portion of the sky. If one were to look closely enough, they could make out its peaks and craters with a naked eye.

"Tis the nearness of Tiber, our largest moon. And also, the number of moons—more light, shows more colors." Wrapping my arms around him, I leaned over his shoulder to kiss his cheek. "And let us not forget the most important bit of all, majicks."

It was three more slumbers before the suns returned—and with them, Caleb awoke to find he had a cute baby bump. We laid there in bed, rubbing his belly and marveling at the proof of our fertility.

Caleb met my eyes with a frown. "If we were in my world, I would be able to calculate how far along I am. I literally have no idea here. Wolf omegas normally have a three-month gestation, but it feels like I've been pregnant nearly that long, and yet I'm just now showing. And not only am I showing, I'm popped out pretty good. With no accurate sense of time, how am I supposed to know how long we have until the baby comes?"

I thought about that for a second then shook my head. "I have no answer to that, mate. The younglings come when they are ready. That is just how it works."

Caleb blew out a breath as he sat up and swung his legs over the side of the bed. "That is such a pat answer, and I get that it's the best you can give me, but it's just so… ugh. It's just frustrating is what it is. I went to sleep with a flat belly, and I wake up with a full-on baby bump. What happens next? Will I go to sleep and wake up in labor? I don't mind not having a flat belly for a good portion of the pregnancy, but I hope it doesn't either rush by before I can blink or take an eternity where I'm waddling around with a watermelon pressing on my bladder."

I could feel his agitation, and hear it in our heartsong—but I had no comfort to offer. After we had dressed, I caught his hand in mine and led him out to the kitchen. I had thought to make him breakfast, but Pinky had the table covered with an array of delicacies. It had taken her several slumbers, but she had figured out how to recreate the pancakes and oatmeal that he had enjoyed at home. He had been too excited by the appearance of familiar foods to question where they came from. When I tried to explain that all of our flour came from the same poppy thistle grain, he had laughed as though I were pulling his leg.

"Score. This tea tastes just like that special herb you used to slip me at home. Would you like a cup?" Caleb held the teapot poised over my empty cup, waiting for my nod to fill it.

I smiled and tipped my chin toward the cup. "Yes, please. You will find that the sunfresh herb grows in abundance here. Those plants in the windowsill over the sink are all sunfresh." Pinky turned a somersault in the air and buzzed over the sink to pluck an orange leaf from a plant. She flew right back over to the table and hovered in front of Caleb, holding the leaf out like an offering for him to sniff.

He set the teapot aside to take the leaf. "Thank you, pretty one. This smells delicious." She chittered excitedly and moved to her favorite spot over his left shoulder, buzzing there like a hummingbird while he examined the leaf. "I love the colors of your flora and fauna. Is this an edible?"

He blushed and shook his head with embarrassment. "Never mind, what am I asking? Of course it's edible or you wouldn't put it in my food and drink. Let me rephrase that. Is the leaf itself okay to eat or does it need to be steeped or something?"

I chuckled and smiled at his adorable blush. "I understood what you meant. And no, it does not need to be steeped. Some people even candy the leaves. My mother does, for example." At the mention of my mom, Caleb paled and looked down at the table.

Hmm. This was not the first time I had noticed his discomfort at the mention of my family, but I could not imagine why. "Caleb, why do you look so worried when I speak of my family? Were you hoping to have me all to yourself? I can keep them away if that is the case. I love my family, but you are the most important thing to me now."

He shook his head and took a tentative taste of the leaf. His face lit up as the sweet flavor flooded his mouth. I waited to see his eyes when the savory back note hit his taste buds. When his eyelids fluttered shut, I was not disappointed. After he had finished, his eyes opened again and he visibly gulped before speaking.

"No… it's not that. Not really. I don't want to keep you away from your family. I think it just gets scarier with every day that passes without me meeting them. I'm settling in and getting so comfortable, but what if they hate me? I've heard so many stories of evil mothers-in-law, you know? If your mom doesn't like me, it could cause a problem in our relationship. And with you guys living for centuries, that's a long time for me to coexist with someone who doesn't like me."

He sighed heavily, then explained a little further. "I have so few memories of what a family even looks like, aside from Helena. It scares me because I'm not sure I'll know how to fit in. What if I don't?"

The sorrowful notes coming from his heartsong brought a pang of sadness to my chest. I reached out and covered his hand with mine. "First of all, it is *us* guys now, remember? You will belong at my side for as long as we live. As for my mother, I promise that she will adore you. If on the off chance that she did not, there would not be a choice—you will always come first for me. But there will be no need to choose, I am confident when I say that my family will adore you. Please do not be nervous, mate. Trust me. Besides, you will see soon enough. As for fitting in, please put that worry aside. You will always fit at my side. You are my mate, the fates themselves have deemed that we are meant to be together, how could you not fit into my family when you are my world?"

He nodded quietly and took a sip of tea. After a moment, he shot me a curious look. "What did you mean when you said we would live for as long as we wish? Doesn't immortality mean that we literally will never die?"

I shook my head. "Yes and no. We Fae age slower than the humans, but we do age eventually. When our bodies get tired, we are the ones who choose when it is time to pass over to the Summerlands and begin anew in a fresh form. It usually takes at least a millennia or two before we reach that point. But eventually, we all must make the decision."

Before I could explain any further, there was a sharp knock at my door. Pinky did an excited somersault and started to buzz off toward the door but I moved faster. "Thank you, little one. But I will answer the door. You go ahead and stay with Caleb." She chittered happily and went back to my mate while I went to answer the door.

"Riley of the Hearthstone clan. What an honor to find you on my doorstep so early in the morning. Welcome, please come in." A woman who lived across town on the other side of Honeymeade was standing on my doorstep.

She and her wife were getting up there in age and I was unsurprised to see a fresh line of wrinkles across her forehead. It would not shock me if I were to hear of the two of them making their own trip to the Summerlands before long. Not because she was looking older, but her eyes had that tired, worn sheen that only came when we began to tire of our existence on this plane.

She shook her head, wrapping her arms around her waist as if she felt a chill. "No, thank you. I hate to disturb you when you are settling into life with your heartsong, but I could not think of anywhere else to turn."

I felt his presence at my back before Caleb walked around to take his place at my side. He smiled at Riley and held out a hand. "Hello, my name is Caleb. Are you sure you wouldn't like to come in and have a cup of sunfresh tea with us?"

As Riley shook his hand, I could tell by the sparkle in her eyes that she was instantly charmed by him. Still, she shook her head. "I apologize, but I really cannot stay long. I am watching a youngling, Hailee is her name. Her grandmother asked me to look after her while she went to look for distant kin in the region just past Sproutville. As you know, her grandmother has been approaching her third millennia."

Riley lowered her voice and looked from side to side as if to make sure that nobody was listening who might judge. "As much as she loved Hailee, it was time for her to pass to the Summerlands."

Caleb gasped. "But what about her granddaughter? Surely she wouldn't want to leave her alone?" He paused, then went still as he correctly read the look on Riley's face. "Wait. You said loved, as in past tense. Is the grandmother gone? How does that work? I thought Fae were immortal."

Riley nodded solemnly. "We are not quite as fragile as the humans, but we can be killed and taken before we are ready to enter the Summerlands. Word has come that the poor dear was attacked by a passing gang of unseelie thugs while she was crossing the neutral zone. Hailee is now alone in the world, but my wife and I cannot keep her. We have our own journey planned to the Summerlands after the next few solstices. So you see, we cannot care for the girl if we will not be here to see it through."

She turned to me with an imploring look on her face. "I have not been able to find anyone in the village who would be willing to take the youngling in. She is a sweet girl, and I hate to see her suffer. My wife remembered that you had shown the girl a kindness recently. Rumor has it that you gifted her a pocket full of gold when she was begging for change in the town square. I thought perhaps if you were willing to do that, there was a chance that you might be willing to take her in."

My heart immediately said yes, but my mind reminded me that I had my own youngling on the way and a new mate who might not want to take another child on to raise. I should have known better because Caleb immediately turned and clutched my arm as he gazed at me with troubled eyes. "Go get her, Tobias. Please bring her home so that we can welcome her into our family. I would go with you, but I think Pinky and I would be better served by staying home and preparing the guest room for our new youngling."

As soon as he spoke, I remembered that Caleb and Helena had met as foster children. Of course my mate would want to open our home to an orphan. Had he not once been one himself? I bent to brush a kiss over his forehead. "As you wish, mate. I will go collect her now."

Riley's face lit up with relief. "You will take her then? Wonderful. Let us go." She lowered her voice again and finally admitted the truth. "It is not that we do not like the girl, but we feel as though her luck is bad. The kind of bad luck that invites the unseelie to one's door." She gave Caleb a final nod, then turned and began to walk down our front path, as if expecting me to follow.

I shook my head at the stupidity of her reasoning, then bent and kissed Caleb again. "I will be back as soon as I can. Thank you, I promise you will love her. I cannot say what it was, but when I last saw her, I felt such affection for the dear youngling. I am pleased that we are able to give her a home."

Pinky was buzzing around excitedly, flipping somersaults beside Caleb's head. Caleb giggled when her skirt tickled his ear, but he kept the presence of mind to give me a shove. "Hurry up and go get our new youngling. No offense, but that Riley woman is a piece of work. I want you to get our new daughter away from her as soon as possible."

I could not agree more. I could hear Pinky chittering excitedly as Caleb closed the door behind me. I was half afraid of what Pinky would create in the way of the bedroom for Hailee, but I had every confidence that Caleb would make sure it wasn't completely over the top.

Then I chuckled to myself and rethought that notion as I caught up with Riley and remembered the pink canopy that Caleb and Pinky had installed over the nursery crib the day before. Hopefully, the youngling Caleb carried would indeed be a girl—and if not, a boy who genuinely adored pink.

CALEB

*H*ailee was a joy and fit right into our household. I had no idea how old she was since the Fae had no reliable method of timekeeping, but she seemed to be about six or seven in human years. She was the sweetest thing, with a sharp mind and a bubbling laugh that mirrored her naturally joyous nature.

Of all the blessings in my life, finding Helena had been among the best. I could only hope that I could pay it forward by providing Hailee with the same strong sense of family that I'd shared with my bestie.

She was already calling us Papa Caleb and Papa Tobias, at my request. I wanted her to know that we were her forever family now and she was safe. In my world, we'd have had to deal with child services and adoption law, while the Fae apparently just took younglings in and that was that. It was weird, but I wasn't about to argue since it worked well in our favor in this instance.

I adored her cute, freckled face. The pointy ears fit her well, giving her an impish look that was only highlighted by her lavender-blue eyes. There was a lot to be done to help her, but I was excited to give her a family life. Her elderly grandmother hadn't had her in school, she hadn't been able to afford properly fitting clothes… it was heartbreaking.

The child's hair had been greasy and uncombed, making me wonder who'd last shown her proper care. My opinion of Riley and her mate had plummeted when I'd seen the girl. Surely they could've at least handled basic grooming for the girl. No matter, she was ours now and we would give her all the love and care that a child deserved.

Pinky was now dividing her time between the two of us, much to Tobias's relief. After a few days that seemed to speed by, we thankfully had a spate of long nights. Even that super huge moon no longer freaked me out, which was a sure sign that I was settling into my new world.

I loved it here, and not just because I was alive and healthy. My bond with Tobias grew stronger every day. Now that we were here, our heartsong was in perfect sync. When he was happy or upset, excited or depressed… I could hear it in the melody that ran between us like a visceral fiber or cord. And the more time we spent together, the more I fell for his quick wit, easy charm and good looks.

Yeah, I was pretty sure I was the luckiest man ever born. The only downside was that every time I woke up, my belly was that much bigger. It was as though I'd skipped over a good month's worth of pregnancy over the course of a few short slumbers—as Tobias called them. I found the whole *time* thing confusing, but I just chalked it up to magic and left it at that.

Pinky took Hailee off for her evening bath while Tobias and I played a game with multi-sided dice cubes. After he beat me for the fourth time, I realized that my head wasn't in it—either that or my luck was shit tonight.

Tobias put the dice away then came over and sat beside me, wrapping his arms around me as he kissed the top of my head. "What is wrong, mate? You do not seem like yourself tonight. Is it the pregnancy?"

I considered it for a moment then shook my head. "No, not really. I just feel itchy in my own skin. I'm not sure what it is, but I need to get in touch with myself and something is blocking me."

We sat there for a few moments before Tobias jumped up and reached for my hand. "I know what the trouble is, mate. You have not changed forms since you came to my world. Why do we not go for an evening run? You can race through the meadows in your wolf form, while I fly along beside you."

That sounded like so much fun. I hesitated for a moment as I considered it. "What about the baby? Do you think it's safe for me to shift this far into the pregnancy? I've never really been around many other pregnant shifters, and never this far along. I honestly have no idea if I should do that or not."

Tobias shrugged. "I cannot think of a reason why it would hurt. If anything, I think it would be good for you. If you are feeling itchy in your skin, perhaps it is simply because your wolf wants out to play."

That was all I needed to hear. After I checked in with Pinky and let her know that she was in charge of the youngling while we went for a walk, Tobias and I stepped outside. I started to undress, but remembered Sammy's words and instead thought my clothes away as I shifted to my wolf.

I was amazed when my clothes simply disappeared during the shift. Although, I wasn't entirely sure that I could even really call it a shift anymore. It was more like I'd simply morphed from one form to the other with a mere thought. Tobias fluttered in the air above me while I ran around in circles chasing my tail and enjoying the feeling of the cool night air ruffling my fur.

It made me happy that we had chosen a time when the moons were present for my first shift. There was nothing like a nighttime run. I opened my mouth to bark at Tobias, when the word *Hey!* came out instead. I tried it again, barking three times, only to hear *Hey! Hey! Hey!* instead. I was so shocked that I jerked backward and fell right on my butt. Tobias landed on the ground beside me, holding his stomach as he laughed.

"Hey yourself, mate. Was that not what you meant to say? You seemed rather surprised there." Tobias's eyes gleamed with humor. The big brat. He knew damn well why I'd reacted like I did.

I answered without thinking, surprising myself all over again when my normal voice came from my wolf's throat. "I meant to bark, but I guess the bark was the equivalent of the word hey? This is what Sammy meant by making sure I spoke to you in this form. Is it me, or is it weird to hear my voice coming from my wolf?"

Even as I spoke, my eyes were caught on the rippling muscles Tobias had on display. I'd been so busy changing myself, I hadn't realized that he had removed his shirt. *Damn, my mate is hot.* Tobias winked at me, then shot straight up in the air. He hovered a few feet over my head as if taunting me while he turned a somersault like Pinky was so fond of doing.

I barked—only to yell out *hey* again—and took off running after him when he flew away. He led me over a meadow of grass, and down a dirt path that took us beside the pond. The field where we'd met Pinky was nothing but grass, now that the flock of fairies had moved along. I chased him over the grass, thrilled to find that I could jump higher and run faster than I ever had before.

At one point, I jumped so high that I easily tackled Tobias and knocked him from the air. Tobias caught me in his arms and I could feel the heady magic in the air as he slowly floated us to the ground. "I hate to scold you, mate. But if you had fallen from that height, you might have hurt yourself or our youngling. Please try not to worry me like that, all right?"

I leaned forward and licked his cheeks, making him chuckle—even though he wiped it away with the back of his hand. I stared at him for a moment before voicing to him the next thought that came to mind. "Wait. People can get hurt here?"

Tobias looked around then leaned very close to whisper in my ear. His voice was so soft, that even a shifter would've confused it with a switch of the wind. "Yes. We can. And that is why we are so careful to avoid... well, we dare not name them but read my mind." He touched his forehead to mine and strangely enough, I was able to see the word he thought into existence within my brain. *Unseelie.*

I gasped. "I've heard of them. Isn't that who Riley said attacked Hailee's grandmother?"

Tobias looked around uneasily. "They are not to be messed with, my love. They will not come here unless called by their name being spoken too many times. They prefer the darker nature of their own kingdom. While ours is light and rainbows... theirs is... well... let us just say it is quite the opposite. Darkness and fear are the rule of the day there. You should be safe, but it is best that you stay at my side until you become acclimated to this world."

Shaking my head, I couldn't help but speak my thoughts. "Great. Now I have another thing to worry about besides meeting the in-laws. Yay, me." When I saw the anguish cross through his eyes, I leaned forward and licked his cheek again. "But also? Yay me because I have you for my mate. Now come on, race me home."

We were both laughing as we ran like children, racing over the meadow and across the dirt path that led us back to

Honeymeade. When we got home and it was time to shift back, I tested the whole morphing thing by picturing my favorite pajamas as I shifted. I couldn't help but laugh when they instantly appeared on my body as I morphed into human form again. I grinned at Tobias and threw my arms around his waist as I stared up at him. "I can *so* get used to this."

TOBIAS

$\mathcal{S}$nuggled up behind my mate in a post-coital bliss—our bodies stuck together thanks to the energy lock—was my favorite place to be. He fit so perfectly in my arms with his back flush against my chest as I stroked a possessive hand over his large belly.

Caleb held his hand out, marveling at the vibrant green aura glowing from his skin. "I don't think I'll ever get over this whole energy thing. Why is it green this time? Last time it was blue, but the first time we were locked together it was purple. Are we cycling through the rainbow? If so, can I just ask that we skip yellow? I'm pretty sure that might make us both look a little jaundiced."

My chest shook with laughter as I bent to kiss his bare shoulder. "We cannot request what color our aura will be, mate. The colors reflect our feelings. The purple was reflective of the mixture of lust, new love, and that sense of wonder we shared during our first mating. The blue aura we saw last time was probably showing the love that has been building between us. I can only think this green we are seeing now is indicative of how peaceful we feel tonight after that moonlit run."

Caleb looked back over his shoulder to catch my eye. "Why does it sound like you're guessing here?"

I nipped at his earlobe, smiling when he squirmed. "Probably because I am? Have you forgotten that this is my first mating? I only know the basics of the energy lock and how we glow afterward, and that the aura is indicative of emotions. As for the rest, I can only assume we will learn as we go."

Caleb flashed me a wink. "So what you're saying is that you Fae literally have afterglow on lockdown." He was silent for a moment then began to chuckle. "When we have our first argument, I'm giving you permission right now to drag me like a caveman into the closest private room and fuck me angrily against a wall."

"I should probably be frightened to ask this—but why, pray tell, are you giving this blanketed permission for me to take you during a moment of ire?"

"Why? Why not? It will be hot as heck, for one thing. And for another, I'm dying to see what color would show up in the afterglow. Would it be bright red for the anger, or would it be a murky gray? Maybe a pink instead of red, because surely our anger would have faded a little during our passion?" Caleb shrugged a shoulder. "I just thought it might be fun to experiment."

I made a humming noise and hugged him closer against me as I kissed along the column of his neck. "I am certainly willing to try. I cannot imagine us ever being that angry with each other, but if the day ever comes then I will be happy to fulfill this request. If for no other reason than the fact that it will likely be a quick road to any necessary reconciliation."

Our heartsong was soft and sweet right now, another sign of our current mood. Now that Caleb was feeling so relaxed,

I decided to ask why he was so nervous about meeting my family. I thought about gleaning the information from his mind, but that felt too invasive. I laid there for a moment enjoying the green aura covering our joined bodies and listened to that beautiful heartsong before I spoke.

"Caleb, my love. I am concerned by the stress I felt from you earlier when we discussed my family. I worry for the youngling, but I am also unhappy to see you suffer. Is there anything I can do to set your mind at ease? Perhaps it would help if you told me more about your worries?" My tone was soft as I kissed him behind the ear. I wanted him to know that I was here for him and genuinely cared about his feelings.

He was silent for a long moment. I watched our aura change slightly as spikes of teal began to pulse over the surface while our heartsong picked up a faster beat. It was still a happy sound, but I could feel the undercurrents of tension that were driving the newly increased rhythm.

I slowly stroked my hand over his belly and kissed the spot where I had bitten him during our first joining. "Talk to me, love. I want to know how you feel."

"I guess I'm just..." His voice trailed off as he blew out a long breath. "Shit. Forgive me. I'm probably just freaking myself out. I'm not usually nervous when meeting new people, but this is your family. These people and their opinions actually matter. I know you said that you would choose me over them if they didn't like me, but how would I feel to put you in that position? Not very good, I can tell you that much. When I made the decision to leave my world, it seemed so easy, you know? Stay there and die, or come here and have true love and a family of my own. Easy choice, right? And yet... not so much."

"Aye, it probably felt like a simple decision at the time. But I can imagine how hard it has been for you to leave everything you know behind. Everything here is new and exciting, but I know that part of you is also missing what you left behind. Whenever I would spend too much time in your realm in the past, I could easily pop home to visit my family if they were not already there with me. And even if my family were with me, I would grow to miss my world after too much time spent in yours. I would grow to miss the colors here, and the richer air. It has been too many slumbers to count since I freely crossed worlds on a whim, but I remember the feeling well."

Caleb relaxed a little, our aura turning back to a pure green as his tension began to ease. "That's probably a lot of it, now that you mention it. I do miss my world. Heck, I miss knowing what time it is and what day it is and... yeah... pretty much all of that. Don't get me wrong, I also love it here. And how petty would I be to resent the chance to have a fantastic life with you in this amazing world, not dying young of a brain tumor? And yet... I find myself stressing out about whether or not your family will like me and missing Helena. I don't think about it all the time. Especially when I'm busy with Hailee and spending time with you. But it's in my quiet moments when the fear creeps in."

"Aww, my poor mate. I hate to think of you feeling that way. There is nothing wrong with being homesick, missing Helena, or being worried about meeting new people. But a problem shared is a problem halved—I cannot help carry your burdens if you do not share them with me. I will not be so foolish as to tell you that your concerns are less than valid, you are allowed to feel however you must. I can promise, however, to listen to your woes and hold you in my arms while I promise to love and cherish you."

Caleb looked back over his shoulder. "The only thing I don't like about being locked in this position is that I can't just kiss you whenever I want. So how about you leaning in here and laying one on me, angel boy? I need to taste your lips after a sweet statement like that one."

"I am always happy to be of service to my mate," I said with a wink as I leaned forward to kiss him as requested.

Things seemed a little better the next day—until I walked into the kitchen and found Caleb on his hands and knees scrubbing the floors while Pinky fluttered around the room making everything else shine as though it were brand new.

Hailee was sitting at the table, practicing her sums on an abacus I had purchased for her. She was chewing on the end of her long braid while she stared at the contraption with frustration. I started to walk into the room when Pinky came flying at me and waved her hands as she chittered indignantly in my face.

I groaned and took a step backward, holding up my hands. "Calm down, fairy girl. I was not going to dirty up his clean floor. I want to make sure that Caleb is not tiring himself. The youngling is due before much longer." Pinky darted away from me, soaring down toward Caleb in a deep arcing swoop until she hovered inches from his nose. He rolled his eyes as she chittered at him. He didn't need to understand her language to pick up on her fussing.

Caleb looked around Pinky to catch my eye. "Did you really need to go and get her all wound up? You know how my pretty girl worries about me."

"As well she should, mate. Why are you doing this when you and I both know that Pinky could have the floor cleaned with a snap of her fingers and a touch of pixie dust?" While I waited for Caleb to answer, Hailee set her work aside to watch us with an interested grin. I flashed her a wink. "I would love to see how your work is coming along, missy. But

I dare say that Pinky would have my head if I walked on this floor right now."

Hailee giggled and shook her head. "Perhaps if you took your boots off then she would not mind. Have you not considered doing so?"

I stared at her for a couple heartbeats while Caleb began laughing, before finally bending and pulling off my boots. "Hailee, love, I am certain that your sums will be correct because you have just proven yourself to be a genius."

Hailee giggled some more. "No, Papa Tobias. I just have common sense. My grams always said it was the best kind of smarts to possess."

Now that I was free to walk on the floor, I darted over to the table and caught her up in my arms. I held her over my head as I spun her in a circle. "Your grams was certainly an insightful woman. Now tell me how much work you have left so that we can help Caleb finish this floor." She was still giggling as I set her back on the chair and bent to look at her sheet of homework.

She had not attended school recently, more's the pity. The first thing that Caleb had insisted upon was Hailee's education. Since school was not in session right now, the teachers had given us a thick packet of work for her to do while the other children were on break. The hope was that Hailee would be caught up when school began again after the summer solstice.

"I just finished my last problem, Papa Tobias. I hurried because Papa Caleb promised to show me the image of my Auntie Helena from the human realm." Her lavender eyes were bright with excitement. The charm I had fashioned for Caleb was a favorite of hers.

"If you'll help me up, I'll call it good enough. Perhaps you would be so kind as to dump the bucket of water for me?" Caleb stood up on his knees and reached for my hands.

Ignoring that, I scooped him up into my arms and carried him back to the table with me. I sat down with Caleb on my lap, while Hailee scooted her chair over to enjoy the show as he removed the cord that held the charm from around his neck.

When I saw the bucket lift and float towards the sink, I shook my head at Pinky. "And you wonder why I think you enjoy making me look bad. I swear I was going to empty that bucket as Caleb requested, once we were finished here."

Pinky wrinkled her nose at me and went about putting away the cleaning supplies with just a snap of her fingers. Caleb had not even lifted the charm to the light before a cup of sunfresh tea was floating across the room to settle in front of him at the table.

I was not entirely joking when I said the little fairy made me look shoddy. Her faithful tending of my mate made it difficult for me to anticipate his needs at times. And yet, I could not resent her presence. Caleb adored her, which was enough for me. Anything or anyone that put that kind of smile on my mate's face was worth having around—even a mouthy fairy with boundary issues.

As we watched the image of Helena and Caleb hugging and heard their words of love echo around the room, Hailee was as entranced as always. She turned to Caleb with shining eyes. "Papa Caleb, do you miss Auntie Helena?"

"With every beat of my heart, little one. Helena will always be a part of me, but she's where she's meant to be and so am I." Despite his honest tone, I couldn't help but pick up a note of sadness in our heartsong.

Resting my chin on his shoulder, I kissed his cheek as I murmured, "Do you regret your choice, my love? If it had not been necessary to save your life, do you think you would have made the same decision?" I hated to sound so needy. But even strong, ancient Fae such as myself were to be permitted our moments of doubt, were we not?

Caleb shifted on my lap until he sat sideways and could put an arm around my neck. "Not for a moment, angel boy. I could never regret a choice that gave me a life with you. Helena and I were in each other's lives for a season, but you were meant to be my forever." He looked down at his belly bump, chewing his lip for a moment before glancing up at me again, that old vulnerability shining from his eyes. "Now if your family would just hurry up and get here, that would be fantastic. As soon as I know that they don't mind a human shifter joining your clan, I will be perfectly at ease."

As soon as he said that, everything clicked. "Is that why you are cleaning so much? I thought perhaps you were nesting in preparation of our youngling. Caleb, my love— you do not need to work to impress my family. They will—" My voice trailed off when I realized there was another presence in the room. Several of them, in fact.

"And what is it that they will be doing, Tobias? Please, do tell. And when you have finished, perhaps you will introduce me to my new son?" My mother was standing there with an indulgent smile on her face and both hands planted on her ample hips.

I bit back a sigh as I shook my head. "Perhaps the first thing they will be doing is learning to knock on my door now that I am mated. But what I was going to say before I was so rudely interrupted—was that my family will love my mate." I rubbed a soothing hand over Caleb's back as I spoke. I could feel his mortification at my family having arrived during such an inopportune moment, not to mention hearing it via the jarring, discordant notes in the heartsong as he quietly panicked.

My mother shook her head impatiently and walked closer to thrust a hand out toward Caleb. As soon as he took it, she covered his hand with the other, sandwiching it between hers as she spoke. "Ignore my son, darling. He means well but the boy has always been a little stiff around the collar. My name is Mitzie. I am the matriarch of the Coppersmith clan. Welcome to our family, dear one. The news of your arrival has spread like a morning mist throughout the realm. We hastened home to greet you, but were delayed by roaming bands of filth who need not be named. I do apologize that it took so long. And sweetest? I am proud to have a strong wolf in our family. I have heard rumors that your wolf is a pure white one—which is rare, if I recall correctly from the days when I was free to walk your world."

Two things happened before Caleb could respond. The first was the warmth I felt spreading over my thighs—and the second was my mother shaking her head as she dropped Caleb's hand and turned to scold me. "Honestly, Tobias. I cannot believe that you were not helping your mate while he was busily nesting. You only need to take a good look at how spick-and-span your house is, to see that this young man has nested but good."

Pinky came buzzing in from where she had been hovering off to the side, chittering nervously as she floated beside Caleb's ear. I was trying to make sense of what was happening when my mother groaned and shook her head again. "Can you not feel the water puddling over your lap and between your feet? The boy's water has broken." She smiled indulgently at Caleb. "I promise that we will laugh about this later over a fine cup of tea, but for now why do we not let my big strong son carry you to bed so that your youngling can come out to greet us?"

I rose in a rush, and nearly slipped on the water that Caleb had spilled. Pinky sent a flash of pixie dust that got Caleb sneezing but kept me on my feet. Screw walking. I let my wings burst forth and cradled Caleb in my arms as I flew straight back to our bedroom. I started to worry about Hailee, but I heard my father and siblings introducing themselves to her. Good. Now I could focus on my mate.

My mother was rushing in behind me. She chattered while she waited for me to get Caleb settled on the bed. Pinky fussed around, fluffing pillows and helping me get him undressed. Where I would have tugged his clothes off, she made his pants vanish with a snap of her fingers. Caleb turned bright red and started to cover his private parts, then let out a loud groan as he doubled over in pain, clutching his stomach with all thoughts of modesty apparently forgotten.

When I started to pull him into my arms, my sister appeared out of nowhere and tugged me aside while my mother pushed her way in. "Let Mom handle it, you big goof. What do you know about birthing younglings?"

I shook my head. "No, Breanne. My place is here with my mate. I know that you normally assist Mother with birthings, but not this time. Go and introduce yourself to your new niece, Hailee. Caleb and I have adopted her as our own. I will tell you the story later, but for now, you go and keep Father and our brothers out of here and set Hailee's mind at ease. I will not have her frightened or sick with worry in this moment."

My mother had already started checking things out with Caleb, but paused long enough to look at me in dismay. "Tobias! You know that you are not meant to be here in the birthing chamber. This is a private moment for the carrier while the sire is supposed to be out bragging and telling anybody who will listen that he is about to be a father."

I took a deep breath before I was tempted to say a few choice words. "Tradition be damned, I will not be leaving my mate's side. He is in a strange new world and has never met you, before the last few heartbeats. It will be far better for him to have me here then to be stressed out while dealing with pain." I knelt down beside the bed, reaching for Caleb's hand. "Not to mention the fact that wild stallions could not drag me from this room. I will not miss the first sight of my youngling greeting the world."

My mother took one look at the love shining in Caleb's eyes as he heard my words and gave a quick nod. "Very well. Then you work to keep Caleb calm and coach him when I say to push and we will get through this together."

CALEB

I don't know why I was shocked when Tobias insisted on staying—even to the point of standing up to his mother and sister—but I was relieved when he climbed onto the bed and settled in behind me.

Throughout my labor, he wiped my forehead with a cool, damp cloth that he'd produced from thin air and encouraged me to push. No matter how much I yelled at him and cursed his mighty glowing cock and its sparkly damned seed—he stayed practically serene while he coached me through the pain.

At the end of a series of pushes that felt like I was trying to push my brain through my birthing canal, Mitzie was pulling an actual baby out of my body. I couldn't help the nervous giggles that erupted as I watched Pinky sever the umbilicus and clean our baby with just a flick of her fingers while Mitzie cooed at her granddaughter as she held her up over her head. I swear to the gods but it looked like a Fae version of the *Lion King* and our daughter was Simba.

When the moment went on a little too long, Tobias loudly cleared his throat. "All right, enough of that, Mother. You will get your time with her but I believe my mate has the right to hold our daughter first."

Mitzie blushed and sent me a contrite smile as she carried our daughter over and laid her on my chest. "Congratulations on the birth of your daughter, sweetums. She looks perfect in every way. Have you chosen a name yet?"

I glanced back at Tobias and he nodded his agreement with the girl's name I'd suggested. I blinked back tears and smiled at the baby I was cradling against my chest as I spoke in a hushed voice. "Yes, this is Emily."

Tobias leaned over my shoulder to rub the crook of his finger over Emily's soft cheek. "Welcome to the world, Emily of Clan Coppersmith."

I was about to ask if we should think about dressing and diapering her when Mitzie looked to Tobias. "Are you ready to do the honors, sweetheart?"

"Honors? What honors?" I asked in confusion. Surely putting a diaper on wasn't an honor. Although, maybe the first time was? What did I know...

"Just lay her on the bed between your legs, sweetums." Mitzi directed me, while she went on to explain what was happening. "The majicks must be brought forth by the youngling's sire before sunset on the day of birth to seal the forms. She won't change forms again until she's older, but she must have the initial morphing for the majicks to take root." As she spoke, Mitzie was already heading toward the door. "Let me call the rest of the family, we would not want them to miss this important moment."

I strained to look over my shoulder, gazing at Tobias in dismay. "Please don't let your family come in here while I'm half naked. I would die!" Before Tobias could respond, I turned back just in time to watch as Pinky tossed pixie dust over my lap. Pajama pants immediately covered my legs, putting me at ease as I leaned forward to lay Emily between them.

Mitzie came back in the room with Breanne, Hailee, and four strange men. I assumed they were the rest of the family, but ignored them for now—I had all the time in the world to meet them. Right now was Emily's moment.

Tobias climbed out from behind me and knelt beside the bed. He stretched out a hand to touch her forehead with a glowing fingertip. White light spread from the spot he touched to surround her entire body with its shining aura. His voice was filled with pure alpha authority as he spoke a single word.

"Athru."

I watched with delight as Emily morphed into a fuzzy white wolf puppy. Even after Tobias pulled his finger back, the white aura continued to surround her. The fur on her body stood on end from the powerful majicks coating it. Everyone *oohed* and *ahhed* while our little pup flopped about on her back and batted at the air with fluffy paws. Even in this form, she was too new to have much muscle strength.

Mitzie's voice trembled as she spoke with tears streaking down her cheeks. "Morph her back, sweetheart. We cannot keep her long in this form, cute as it may be. She needs to know that human is the base form, after all."

"Athru." As Tobias touched his glowing fingertip to her forehead again, Emily changed forms—but not into a human. This time she morphed into a Fae baby with pointed ears. She screeched with a wailing cry, her tiny eyes squeezing shut as her fists smashed at the air, the white aura moving with her.

I bent to pick her up, intending to provide comfort. But as I lifted her, ethereal wings with the same purple and teal tones of her sire—along with white polka dots that perfectly matched the tone of my wolf's coat—popped out from between her shoulder blades.

Tobias gasped. "Poor wee lass! That is why she was crying; the wings probably burn the first time they extend." He brushed a finger between her wings, while I cradled her against my chest. He must have sent a majick to soothe her, because the white aura flared brighter for a split second, then her cries immediately changed to coos.

Mitzie clapped her hands excitedly while Pinky did a series of aerial somersaults, splashing pixie dust all around. Mitzie crowed with delight, bouncing on her feet as she cheered. "Oh, my! Will you look at that? Our lass will have strong majicks, indeed, if she has three forms. Tis so rare! Even back when we mingled between the realms, it was a rarity, indeed, to see a youngling with more than two forms."

"Athru." As Tobias touched her forehead a final time, Emily's ears rounded again and her wings disappeared into her back—leaving behind twin birthmarks of lacy rosettes. Breanne pushed through the crowd of men with a diaper and a handful of pink clothing.

She stopped beside the bed, her voice hesitant as she looked at me with a hopeful smile. "May I help you dress her for the first time?" I couldn't help but smile when she added a greeting, almost as an afterthought. "By the way, I am Breanne of the Coppersmith clan—as you no doubt heard— and I am meant to be your sister now."

I passed Emily to her aunt as my heart swelled so large that I wondered if it was about to burst out of my chest. "Here, Auntie Breanne. Why don't you cradle your niece and love on her for a moment before you dress her? I think I need a moment."

As she eagerly took Emily into her arms, I finally took a good look at all the faces around the room—faces filled with nothing but welcoming smiles for me and adoration for my daughter.

It hit me all at once that I'd been silly to worry about being accepted. It was like nothing I'd ever had before outside of my parents and Helena. And yet, I could feel the sense of family wrapping around me and telling me that I was one of them, even if I didn't know all of their names yet.

Tobias looked alarmed as I burst into tears and quickly rushed back onto the bed to pull me against his side. Mitzie shook her head with a knowing smile. "Just hug your mate, sweetheart. Caleb's heart is full right now. Those are happy tears we are seeing."

TOBIAS

"*J*ulius, put Pinky down." My idiot brother was holding the poor fairy by the tips of her wings and laughing while she chittered angrily in his face. He was not trying to be mean; the fool had always held a secret adoration of fairies. He had commented many times since they had arrived about the delicate beauty of Pinky's wings and the musicality of her language.

It would not surprise me if this was his way of flirting with poor Pinky. I shuddered at that thought—and the ramifications of my brother mating with a fairy—and began to repeat myself. Before I could say another word, Caleb walked in the room. He took one look at my brother and came charging over.

"I'm sorry, I forget whether you're Julius or Igor, but you really cannot do that to Pinky. She is a sentient being, the same as you or me." Caleb spoke politely, but his eyes were filled with righteous indignation. His hands kept flexing and fisting as if he were fighting to stay calm.

Igor walked in and plucked Pinky from Julius, cupping her in his palms as he held her out to Caleb. "Ignore my twin, he has always been fascinated by fairies. He meant her no harm, I promise. But as you can see, they have good reason to stay away from him."

Pinky blew Igor a flirty kiss before fluttering over to the safety of Caleb's shoulder. My oldest brother, Ignatius—or Nate for short—came strolling into the living room. "Are you twins fecking about with the fairy again? Mom told you not to upset Caleb. You know she is afraid that he will not wish to remain part of our family if you keep upsetting him."

I wished I owned a camera like the humans had to capture Caleb's face in that moment. I thought about working a spell to create a remembrance charm, then thought better of it. The expression would have faded before I had time to create the spell. Besides, it was not as though I would ever forget the look in his eyes when he heard that my mother had the same concerns that he held.

Igor was closer, so he reached out and ruffled Caleb's hair affectionately. "See? We heard that you were worried about us liking you. Funny how that works both ways, is it not?"

I held up my hands when Caleb's eyes shot to mine, as if to ask why I had told my family about his private concerns. "It was probably Pinky's chittering, or what they heard when they arrived. I have not said a word. Pinky, however? That little fairy gossips about anything and everything to anyone who will listen. Just wait until you finally learn her language, you will long for the days when you could not understand her ramblings."

Igor chuckled in agreement, then got a thoughtful look. "We could spell him to understand all the Fae languages. In fact, we should—and I am surprised you have not thought of it yourself—in case he were to get lost and not know how to find his way home again."

Caleb looked intrigued, then turned to me with a bright smile. "Can you do that for me, angel boy? I would love to be able to understand my pretty girl. Oh! Would I be able to converse with her? Or would I have to learn how to speak fairy?"

Igor shook his head. "Oh, no. We can spell you to be fluent in all the languages. Really, it is but a simple matter."

Before Caleb could say anything else, Hailee came running into the room and ran straight over to stop in front of Igor. She looked up at him with a winsome smile, clasping her hands to her chest as she bounced up and down on the balls of her feet. "Uncle Igor, can we go play at the pond while Emily takes her nap? Granny told me to ask you. She said not my other uncles, only you."

Julius clutched his chest as if mortally wounded. "Not your other uncles, eh? Only this lout will do? I think I need to have words with your granny. I will have you know that your Uncle Julius is thrice the fun of your Uncle Igor."

Nate gave Julius a shove. "Are you daft? I do believe that was Mother's point. Boring Igor is the responsible one. We are not to be trusted around younglings, remember?"

Hailee wrapped her arm around Caleb's waist. I smiled as I watched the two of them laughing at my idiot brothers as they began pushing and play-fighting each other. Igor sighed, shaking his head as if he could not believe the level of our brothers' stupidity.

"I am not boring, I am responsible. Remind me, who were the ones that nearly drowned our cousin Edwina in that same pond?" Julius and Nate were too busy shoving each other around to hear Igor at first.

Julius was the first to respond as he broke out with a booming laugh. "Always with Edwina! Surely you are not going to remind us of that old gag? That was centuries ago when we were but younglings ourselves. And let us not forget the important fact that she lived to tell the tale."

Nate nodded along with Julius. "Besides, who knew that

the silly girl would take us seriously when we told her to dive to the deepest part of the lake and count to one thousand before she came back up if she wanted to play hide and seek with us? If she wanted to pretend she was part merfolk, that is on her."

I held up a hand. "How is it on her when you went home for lunch while she was down there counting? If Igor and I had not decided to take an afternoon swim, Edwina might have suffered a different fate."

Igor started cracking up. "I have to question whether her fate was so much better than drowning. That mate of hers is a piece of work. And have you met her thirteen younglings? There are so many of them, they might as well be a flock of fairies."

Julius and Nate started laughing along with him, but I shook my head and tried to explain to Caleb. "They don't like our cousin Myron, Edwina's mate, because he never falls for any of their gags. Also, his majicks are stronger."

Igor snorted. "Of course his majicks are stronger. He is a giant, everything about him is stronger." At Caleb's questioning look, Igor hastened to explain. "He is quite literally a giant. My brothers and I have been trying to understand how they manage to fit—" He paused to shoot a look at Hailee, as if suddenly remembering that he needed to temper his language around the youngling. "What I mean to say is, how they manage to fit in the same bed."

Caleb laughed knowingly. "I'd imagine the fitting into the same bed part probably works like everything else in this world—with a little bit of majick"

"What are you lot talking about?" My dad came in the room and sat down on the couch. He patted the cushion beside him for Hailee to join him as he began peeling a starfruit.

"You don't want to know, George. Is Mitzie done bathing

Emily?" Caleb had grown closer to my dad than anyone else in my family, so far. Probably because my dad was calmer than my brothers and far less inquisitive than my mother and sister.

"Aye, she and Breanne are dressing the lass. I was to tell you that we would love to stay and watch the younglings if you and Tobias would like to have an afternoon away." My dad smiled and held out a piece of fruit to Caleb.

Caleb plucked the fruit from Dad's fingers and popped it in his mouth as he headed out of the room with Pinky flying at his side. "I'll have to check with Tobias, but that sounds like fun to me."

Once he was gone, Igor flashed me a grin. "I like your mate, Tobias. He is a decent sort, but more importantly—he sure adores these younglings. He is a good dad. The goddess was kind to change his fate and offer him a chance to come to this realm. Who would have guessed that your heartsong played within the human world."

Julius nodded in solemn agreement. "You were fortunate indeed, little brother. It pains me to think that you might have never met your heartsong. Sure, you could have taken a mate—but that would have paled next to having your own heartsong."

I had already told my family about the miracle of the portal appearing in my bedchamber and the offer I was given. When they heard about how Caleb had been at death's door when I found him, they had all been horrified. Mom had decided that Caleb was her new child and was on a mission to get him to call her mom. My father was just waiting for Caleb to get comfortable enough to call him dad without being prompted. My brothers and Breanne were placing bets on which one would get their way first.

As for me, I did not care how long it took. I knew it would happen eventually. What I was worried about was whether or not I would ever have a peaceful moment in my own home again. For the past seventeen slumbers since Emily had entered the world, my entire family had spent every waking moment in our house. As much as I loved them, I really need them to get their lives back—and give me mine.

With that in mind, it occurred to me that my mother's offer was a golden opportunity for some alone time with my mate. Maybe if we could have a moment's privacy, it would not bother me so much to have the clan underfoot.

Maybe. My brothers should still probably get back to their own lives if I were to remain sane... but first, I would have an afternoon of solitude with Caleb.

CALEB

*A*s soon as we got outside, it was as though a weight lifted from my shoulders that I hadn't realized was there. Tobias and I hadn't had a moment alone since Emily's birth, and I was excited to spend the afternoon with him. I knew that my girls would be well taken care of with the family, so I was free to just enjoy a date with my angel boy.

I thought my clothes away with a blink as I morphed into my wolf. Tobias knelt beside me, rubbing each of my ears between his thumb and forefinger before he slowly ran a hand down my back. His fingers wove through my fur, then he cupped his hand to brush along the length of my tail. I stood there dancing from foot to foot and preening proudly while my mate admired my wolf.

"Hey!" I laughed all over again at the way my bark became a spoken word. Even the sound of my laughter was enough to make me laugh harder. It was so strange to hear myself laugh in this form. When I got control of myself again, I finally spoke, "Did you have anywhere in mind that you wanted to go today? Your brothers were telling me about the Crystal Falls. Could we go there?"

"That sounds like the perfect place to go. I doubt your wolf will have any problems navigating the rock formations, but if you do, then I will just carry you to the top." As he spoke, Tobias had already removed his shirt and allowed his wings to unfurl.

His wings made a snapping sound then fluttered a few times as he stretched his wings. As he lifted from the ground, Tobias flew in a circle around me before tipping his head toward the east. "Let's go then, my love. Let me show you some of the wonders of your new world."

We ran across the meadow, this time going all the way to the end and beyond. I didn't know if it was the magic in the air, the richer oxygen, or if my wolf had changed somehow in this new land—but I ran faster than I ever had before. It felt like we'd crossed miles in the same space of time that it would've taken me to go a few blocks in my world.

After we crossed through a gorgeous forest of stately purple trees, we came out at the base of a steep hill. The ground was loose, rich soil that I would've expected to sink into, but instead I seemed to spring back up with every step like I was on a trampoline. I was having the time of my life and so focused on the bouncy dirt that I almost missed the rock formations at first.

The shining rocks were actually big chunks of real gems. Amethyst, citrine, ruby, and the clearest of crystals—along with many other sparkly gems that I couldn't take the time to name—grew in the igneous rock formations. I scrambled from rock to rock, weaving between them as the trail grew steeper. Tobias hovered nearby, as if ready to catch me if I stumbled.

"Hey!" I barked up at him. "It's steep, but I've totally got this." Right as I said that my paw stepped wrong and I started to slide as the ground gave out beneath me.

Tobias picked me up with one arm around my middle, lifting me into the air with him as he flew over the falling rocks. "You were saying something about totally having that?"

"Hey!" I chuffed, and groaned when it came out as a giggle. I gave up the fight and snuggled into Tobias's hold as the sound of water hit my ears. Who cared about pretending to be the tough guy when there was something exciting to see?

We flew around a bend in the mountain and there it was —clear blue water spilled over the top of the ridge, pouring straight down about three hundred feet where it fell into a twisting river at the bottom of a ravine. Droplets of water splashed in our faces. The air coming from the falls smelled fresh; it reminded me of melting snow from my world. As I looked down into the ravine, I was suddenly grateful that I had no fear of heights or this adventure would've sucked balls—and not in a good way.

"I will need to hug you a little tighter now because this is a sharp drop we need to make." True to his word, Tobias pulled me closer to his chest, holding me firmly as he wove around behind the falls and dropped straight down into a hidden cavern that was tucked away behind the curtain of water.

As soon as he set me down, I carefully walked toward the edge to peer out through the gaps in the flow. I gasped in delight as my heart thrilled at the view spread out before me. The vibrantly colored, jewel covered hills made me feel like I was standing atop a dragon's hoard. I saw a field of flowers in the distance. It took me a second for it to compute, then I knew they weren't fairies because I could see the buds.

I shifted to my human form before I turned to look over my shoulder at Tobias with surprise. "I'm afraid to ask how big those flowers are in the distance. I can see the buds! Those must be as big as cars for me to be able to see those from here."

Tobias slipped his arms around my waist as he came up behind me, resting his chin on my shoulder the way he loved to do. "Aye, I reckon they are about the size of a small car. Those are the elephantine blossoms of Sproutville—where the pixies live. I would love to take you there one day, but first we would need to get a day pass. The pixies do not care for drop-ins, and you would not want to see them upset."

As I took that in, I couldn't help but grin that this was my life now. I couldn't wait to see what adventures would come next. As I thought about that, I spun in his arms and wrapped my arms around Tobias's neck. Standing on tiptoe, I stole a quick kiss before leaning back to smile into his eyes.

"Thank you for bringing me here. I was just thinking about how exciting my life is now. But you know what? No adventures I can possibly have here will ever hold a candle to our heartsong." As I spoke, the melody of our unique song wrapped around us. We stood there smiling at each other for a long moment while our hearts pounded in rhythm with the music the two of us created.

Tobias brushed a kiss over my forehead before speaking in a husky voice. "Does that mean you are still glad you said yes?"

"Are you kidding? My mama didn't raise no fool. Saying yes to you was the best thing that ever happened to me. I can't help but think that life itself is the biggest adventure now. I'm pretty sure that no matter what might come our way, we will be able to handle it together. Our daughters, our pet stalker fairy, and the crazy family that came along with you—it's all just icing on the cake. You and me? That's the real adventure."

Tobias brushed his lips tenderly against mine for a quick

kiss before pulling back to smile. "I love you so much, Caleb. Thank you for saying yes and agreeing to come on this adventure with me."

I blinked away happy tears as our heartsong sped up into a joyous crescendo. "Thank *you* for stepping through the portal and agreeing to the challenge that set all of this in motion. Now how about you magic us up some food and we have a romantic picnic before we go home to rescue our girls from Mom and Dad?"

Tobias barked out a laugh. "You totally called them Mom and Dad! Wait until I tell Breanne that she was the winner. She was the one that laid odds on you calling them that at the same time rather than picking one or the other. Igor did too, but he thought it would take at least another ten slumbers. Breanne had it as happening within the next two or three at the most." He froze, as if realizing that I wasn't supposed to know about the silly wager.

I rolled my eyes as I laughed along with him. "I hope they knew—as you should have, as well—that I was aware of that bet. I forgot myself just now or I wouldn't have said it. I was trying to hold off a little longer."

Tobias looked a little bit shocked. "How did you know? Did Pinky tell you? Wait, it could not have been her since you do not understand her language yet."

"I feel like I should tease you, but I'm really hungry so I'm just going to remind you that I'm a shifter—a wolf shifter with superior hearing. If you and your siblings want to keep a secret from me, you should probably leave the house before you discuss it."

Tobias cracked up as he lifted me by the waist and spun me in a slow circle. "How about we keep that secret to ourselves? It might come in handy for you to be able to over-hear some of the nonsense my siblings try to concoct."

"I can work with that," I said with a wink as he lowered

me to the ground. I gave him a swat on the butt then squealed as he tried to get me back. "If you want to fool around, you'd better conjure up a blanket and some food first. I need a clean place for us to sit and some food in my belly."

"Aye. A demanding little thing, are you?" Tobias flashed me a wink as he snapped his fingers and a picnic blanket appeared on the ground, complete with pillows for us to recline against. Another snap provided an overflowing picnic basket. He took my hand and led me over the blanket, pulling me down onto his lap as he reached for the basket. "As it happens, I happen to adore demanding little things. What can I give you next?"

I wrapped my arms around his neck again and snuck a kiss before answering. "Just a little bit of food, there's nothing else I need. I have your love and our family—what else could I possibly want?"

Tobias winked and held a chocolate covered strawberry to my lips. I moaned and took a bite, closing my eyes as its succulent sweetness overpowered my taste buds. After I swallowed, I ate the rest of the berry in a single bite before turning back to him.

"You're right, chocolate totally works. I will always want chocolate." I laughed as he leaned forward to lick the juices from my lips before kissing me soundly.

When he broke the kiss, Tobias pressed his forehead against mine. "Then you shall always have chocolate, my love. Anything you want or need is yours to have—forever."

As he continued to hand-feed me while we looked out at the view through the waterfall, I listened to the melody of our heartsong and gave thanks one more time for all the gifts in my life—including life itself.

Not only had I been blessed with a longer life than I ever

could have foreseen—I would be spending it with the one man who literally made my heart skip a beat in rhythm with his own. Talk about your grand adventures.

ABOUT THE AUTHOR

Thank you for reading this book. Every story I write has a piece of my heart attached. Here's a little bit about me… I'm a happily married mom of one snarky teenage boy, and three grown "kids of my heart." As a reader and big romance fan myself, I love sharing the stories of the different people who live in my imagination. My stories are filled with humor, a few tears, and the underlying message to not give up hope, even in the darkest of times, because life can change on a dime when you least expect it. This theme comes from a lifetime of lessons learned on my own hard journey through the pains of poverty, the loss of more loved ones than Iâ€™d care to count, and the struggles of living through chronic illnesses. Life can be hard, but it can also be good! Through it all I've found that love, laughter, and family can make all the difference, and that's what I try to bring to every tale I tell.

Would you like to receive my newsletter?
Click Here for a free book and the option to sign-up for
News from the Nest.

Facebook reader group: The Hawke's Nest

ALSO BY SUSI HAWKE

Written as Susan Hawke

How Not To Blend

How Not To Tuck

How Not To Sin

How Not to Break

Written As Susi Hawke

Northern Lodge Pack Series

Northern Pines Den Series

Blood Legacy Chronicles

Legacy Warriors Series

The Hollydale Omegas

MacIntosh Meadows Series

Lone Star Brothers Series

Collaborations

Three Hearts Collection (with Harper B. Cole)

Waking The Dragons (with Piper Scott)

Team A.L.P.H.A. (with Crista Crown)

Rent-A-Dom (with Piper Scott)

Alphabits (with Crista Crown)

Rescued

Abduction

Conversion

Check out my audio books!

Susi Hawke on Audible

Susan Hawke on Audible

40765738R00090

Made in the USA
Middletown, DE
31 March 2019